JUST TOSS THE ASHES

JUST TOSS THE ASHES

By Marta Merajver Kurlat

Translation by Gretta K. Siebentritt

Jorge Pinto Books Inc.
New York

Just Toss the Ashes

By Marta Merajver Kurlat

Copyright © 2005 Marta Merajver Kurlat

Copyright of the translation © 2007 by Jorge Pinto Books Inc.

Originally published in Spanish with the title *Gracias por la Muerte*, January 2006 by Jorge Pinto Books

All rights reserved. This book may not be reproduced in whole or in part, in any form (beyond copying permitted by Sections 107 and 108 of the United States Copyright Law, and except limited excerpts by reviewer for the public press), without written permission from Jorge Pinto Books Inc. 212 East 57th Street, New York, NY 10022.

Published by Jorge Pinto Books Inc., website: www.pintobooks.com

Translation by Gretta K. Siebentritt

Cover design by Susan Hildebrand

Cover image: © *Odalisque with a Slave* by Jean-Auguste Dominique Ingres. Licensed by Corbis.com

Book design by Charles King, website: www.ckmm.com

ISBN 978-0-9790766-8-8
0-9790766-8-4

CONTENTS

Chapter 1

THE DISCOVERY

"Mom! I didn't realize you were . . ."

The words caught in his throat. His mother, a light, restless sleeper who woke at the slightest noise, who was furious whenever his voice—and before, his father's—wrenched her from her hard-won slumber, had failed to hear the three keys turning in the lock, the thud of the heavy oak door closing, had not shrieked her accusatory, "You woke me up again! Now how am I ever going to get back to sleep?"

His mother lay in bed, face up, her arms crossed over the girlish nightshirt, pink and dotted with incongruous little blue bears, carefully folded over her chest. He approached her in silence, trying to beat back the familiar sensation halfway between sobs and nausea that began to constrict his stomach. He told himself she was sound asleep, perhaps with the help of a few glasses of wine or some sleeping pills, or both if one or the other had not been enough to induce sleep.

Contemplating her serene face, the skin virtually free of wrinkles, he noticed in particular that the deep furrow that traveled down between her eyebrows when she was consumed by anxiety was so completely smoothed over you would have to guess it was there.

She was resting peacefully. He wasn't about to risk her fury—the fury of a wild animal—by waking her from her deep sleep, maybe even a pleasant one, since she seemed to be smiling faintly. She, who never smiled save for a pained, if not sardonic expression.

He'd leave the bedroom, turn off the bedside lamp. Let her rest. Poor Mom. He'd tell her about it when she woke up in the morning. The news would be a happy corollary to a good night.

He went to his own room, closed the door, and put on some music, keeping the volume low, just in case. He had spent the weekend at the country home of his girlfriend's parents. He was finding it more and more difficult to return home. He was increasingly weighed down by the contrast between that happy atmosphere—where conversation flowed chaotic and frivolous, but always warm towards him—and his own . . . home, if one could call it that, devoid of voices when his mother was not there or resounding with the voices of strangers that reached into every corner from the television set when she returned home in the evening and turned it on while lighting her cigarette, the first step of a ritual in which seeking him out was much lower down on the list.

The CD player's automatic six-disk tray was already set up with his favorites. With the first beats of "I Will Survive"—he and Mom had laboriously deciphered the lyrics . . . he couldn't remember how long ago, after he started high school, during a period when Mom was able to share at least a few things with him—the feeling of nausea resolved into a question that, he now realized, had been going round in his mind since the moment he had seen Sylvia submerged in such peaceful slumber. Why hadn't Mom put on the nightshirt? She was perfectly capable of going to bed in her clothes, or partially dressed, but tonight she was still in her baggy pants, with the nightshirt she hadn't managed to put on . . .

"I'm getting myself all worked up like an idiot," he thought while terrible scenes from the past paraded frenetically through his head. All of that was over and done with. Mom was in good hands, seeing a competent professional who kept her under control and was gradually leading her out of the labyrinth of melancholy, with ups and downs of course, but with the way out guaranteed. Guaranteed in what direction? Mom was often despondent, but she was strong. She'd demonstrated it lots of times, in her incongruous way of doing something, yet all the while insisting "I can't."

But the nightshirt . . . it was out of place. Best to go back and double check and then definitely get some sleep himself until the alarm clock propelled him into the vortex of another Monday morning, the beginning, like all Mondays since he had left behind the calvary of high school, of a busy week full of promise, discoveries, and surmounting obstacles. But first, confirm that Mom was sleeping, at peace with herself and with the world.

Seconds later he was opening the door of their bedroom—he still had a hard time thinking of it as *hers* ever since Dad left—and turning on the overhead light. It was strange. Light never bothered Mom, only sounds.

The three 100 watt bulbs revealed certain details that he had not noticed earlier. Next to Mom, on the pillow, was Plafito, the little stuffed panda he had given her when he was young. She had tripped over some wires from the electric guitar amp tangled in the hall. She had taken a spectacular fall which he (at age, what, ten?) had summarized as a Plaf! Hence the name.

Mom was asleep, sure. Yet she was so still that she appeared not to breathe at all. Her skin looked transparent too, as if the blood had retreated before the light . . . and there were livid spots, like bruises. He desperately needed to hear her fury. He began to call her name, a little louder each time, and to shake her by the shoulders. But Mom did not respond. Her head lolled back, her arms dropped, and she was cold, so very cold. He suddenly realized exactly what kind of peace Mom was resting in. She, who was always saying that death was the only form of liberation, who had tried all kinds of tricks that might enable her to cling to life, who had gone away but had always returned to him, as if he were the only thread pulling her back after all the others had been cut. She, who had attempted to attempt—there was no other way to describe it—to commit suicide, or to live, had managed this time to find the dreamless sleep she so desired. Mom was dead.

It now fell to him to unleash the accusation and the anguish.

Lucas tried to locate his father at the little apartment, a loan from a friend, where he had "temporarily" installed himself after leaving the house. Temporarily, yet six years had transpired. The answering machine picked up. He didn't leave a message. He didn't know how one left such a message. He was surprised, not only that the tears had not come, but because he had very nearly smiled recalling the old joke about not breaking bad news to someone all at once. Perhaps he should call back and explain that "Mom had climbed up onto the roof?" Where could his father be? Impossible to guess. He was totally unpredictable in his comings and goings. The only sure thing about Jaime was that everything was perpetually temporary, just as the only sure thing about this mother—it was clear now—was that sooner or later she would succeed in killing herself.

He was not planning to go back into the bedroom. His childhood horror of all things associated with death, to the point that for years he had held his breath when passing by a cemetery, was exceeded only by the revulsion he felt toward any corpse, even an insect's. That thing on the bed was not his mother, no. Seated before the telephone, his slim, strong body leaning forward as if to grasp the receiver, he suddenly said aloud, "I don't know her." In a searing flash of insight he perceived that he truly did not know the dead woman. He had not really known Sylvia when she was alive and she, in her final act, had deprived him of the opportunity to get to know her in the future.

Now the tears came. Tears of rage: as usual, the bitch had thought only of herself. True to form.

With stiff fingers, he dialed the number again and again. Busy. During several nasty fights between his parents before the separation, Lucas had heard his mother reproach Jaime for his "oral diarrhea." And he suffered from it all right. He also was afflicted with the other kind and both were chronic. His father was a diarrhea-producing factory. It poured out of his mouth, his ass, and his pockets. Words, shit, cash. Always in the wrong place at the wrong time, because it could be any place, any time. Once during an argument, when Jaime had told her to go shit in her hat, Sylvia had retorted, "Living with you, I live submersed in shit." She cut through that shit with her lacerating words, as if with a sharp knife. Lucas bled along with Jaime. But there would be no more words, not that kind or any other. Such as when his mother, indignant, was capable of not speaking to them for days. And now she had opted for an all too eloquent silence.

His rage deepened. Busy. And what the hell was she reproaching him for with the silence of her death?

Lucas had heard—or had he read it in a Sunday supplement?— that suicide was nearly always directed at others. He culled a few disjointed concepts from his memory: revenge, blame, depression, breakdown. But Mom had been improving in recent months. She'd appeared composed, living one day at a time, maybe not as he would have liked, but living nonetheless.

So, what had happened in the two days he was gone? Because something new must have come up, something he hadn't been aware of, a setback in the direction of this—some would say easy—liberation; but triggered by what?

Busy. Son of a bitch. Mom—who was so sophisticated and who Lucas liked to tease with displays of feigned ignorance that appalled her,

(Cortázar? The Colombian guitarist?

What school have we been sending you to? Please!)—liked to quote a phrase from Disraeli: conspicuous by his absence. That would include Jaime too. Erased when he needed him.

He decided to call a truce with the telephone and tried instead to reconstruct that Friday, beginning in the morning and up to the moment when he'd said goodbye to Sylvia.

She had left very early to meet a client before going over to the courts and from there to her office. She'd called him at noon to suggest lunch together downtown, but he'd had to pick up some notes from a fellow student at the university at the exact same time, then take the car to the mechanic, then classes, and then, and then. Mom hadn't sounded upset: "Sure, sure. That's okay. So let's meet for dinner at 8:30 at the Elba. Ciao. I love you lots."

Lucas arrived promptly at the Elba because she hated it when people weren't on time. It was a major source of friction with Jaime for whom, she would say, time was internal and his watch simply a decoration. Sylvia respected the time as if she were British. It was ridiculous to the extreme that her failed suicides had never once interfered with scheduled business or social commitments. Realizing this, one of the psychiatrists with whom she had traversed a stretch of her first depression had imposed an unending list of "tasks" on her with the noble intention of using duty to keep her from death. At first, she clung to this artifice as if it were a life preserver. "Strange," Lucas lost himself momentarily in his memory of the episode. "It actually was to preserve her life." But Sylvia had quickly abandoned it, saying it did not solve the problem, only postponed it. Postponement, procrastination, delay, lateness, lagging were not for her.

When Lucas entered the restaurant, there was his mother, installed at "their" table, one they had occupied with increasing frequency since she, who knows why, had stopped cooking. Absorbed in a book, naturally, her blond hair in disarray and a cigarette butt in her hand; there, but somewhere else too, always somewhere else. Years before, when Lucas wanted to know how she had gone from brunette to blond, her response had puzzled him: "Old ladies like me dye our hair, and when an old lady dyes her hair black, it's the closest thing there is to the witches in the story books." But she wasn't old! Lucas had rebelled then as now, glancing at the menu with one eye and surveying his mother's face with the other. She was only fifty. There were plenty of women her age and older whose looks turned on much younger men. No need to go any farther than Gabriel's mom, who went around half naked . . . no point arguing about it. Mom had made it clear she was born old.

The waiter, "their" waiter, who'd watched him grow and develop in the culinary delights, approached them smiling.

"What are you looking at the menu for? For you only four dishes exist . . . at least here."

A veiled allusion, or maybe not so veiled, to the likelihood that Lucas' selections were different when he dined in more sophisticated venues.

"You're right, Emilio. Today is the steak with mushrooms."

"And for the lady?"

"The grilled pork. With potatoes Provencal."

Sylvia closed the menu and lighted another cigarette. The food would arrive in fifteen, twenty minutes. Plenty of time. The drinks Emilio knew by heart. A half carafe of red for her, no soda no ice. A Coke for Lucas. "Something else, that kid. Doesn't smoke, doesn't drink," he muttered as he headed for the kitchen.

Sylvia made the face that passed for a smile.

"We're not going to mention to him that the only thing you don't drink is wine, eh, Lucky?"

It was a gesture of complicity, but it had sounded negative, like when he was little and she'd scold him. And he bristled at the nickname, because he didn't feel very "lucky." When they were handing out what he considered luck, he hadn't been at the top of the list.

They talked about their day, his upcoming weekend at the farm, about going to the movies together on Wednesday. Mom didn't have any concrete plans for the next two days. She might get together with friends, or maybe get a little work done in the office. Maybe. But there wasn't anything abnormal about that. It had been her routine every weekend since she'd stopped spending them in bed: winter and summer, Friday evening to Monday morning, oscillating between fits of crying and bouts of destruction that propelled her out of bed to break dishes and slash the furniture and walls when his father was still living at home and the two of them would go together to the club, the return trip always clouded by the uncertainty of what might lie in wait for them. Sylvia unconscious, Sylvia drunk, Sylvia submerged in one of those never-ending silences from which she could not be roused, the house upside down as if it had been left to the mercy of an enraged maniac?

He recalled one occasion when she had asked, between screams, to be institutionalized. Jaime had rejected the idea outright.

"Pretending you're crazy isn't worth it. Besides, there isn't any money for that. Where do you want to go, to Moyano?"

Even so, he spoke with the psychiatrist on call, who strongly discouraged such a move.

"No need to be alarmed. She's not going to actually kill herself. She needs to reconnect with reality," he pontificated. "The atmosphere at the public psychiatric hospital isn't going to help her. Try to set up a network of friends and relatives to support her."

But how not to leave her alone when she pushed them away,

rejected them, badgered them ceaselessly, precisely so they would leave her alone. Relatives and friends, forget it. Best they don't even find out about it.

"You so much as open your mouth," the threat was directed toward Jaime, "and you'll never see me again."

And he had obeyed. Lucas wondered whether it had been out of fear or convenience. He knew that the darkest aspects of Sylvia's personality disconcerted his father as much as they did him. He also knew—impossible not to know since the fights always began and ended on the subject—that Sylvia supported the household since, regardless of whether Jaime earned more or less, the money flowed from him along with the diarrhea and he always managed not to have any means with which to pay.

Dinner that Friday evening ended with dessert and coffee on an amiable and companionable note. The short walk to the house took place in silence, but he had taken it as a positive silence, empathetic.

Mom had helped him pack his bag in good humor, with several "don't forget to take . . . ," concerned about what he might need for a two day stay. Then she had hugged him, but nothing out of the ordinary, and said, "Have a wonderful time. I'll lock up."

He had loaded the bag into the car and focused on the new speed limit—terrible, what was the use of having a car that did 300 if they restricted you to 80?—and the prospect of a weekend of sun, swimming pool, barbecue, dogs, which Mom would never allow in the house "because they're too much work," and most of all, Estela. He had to acknowledge that she definitely was his little slice of good luck.

The insistent ringing of the telephone brought him abruptly back to the need to resolve "this." Now everything having to do with Mom was a thing. He answered, silently praying it was Jaime. He did not say hello.

"Dad?"

"Yes, how did you know?"

"I didn't know, I hoped. Dad I have to tell you . . ."

Jaime interrupted him with a drawn out story about the call that had kept his line busy for "hours," never-ending, with detours, and then detours from the detours. True to form.

"Cut it short, Dad," Lucas barked. "Mom killed herself."

There. It was said. Dad's response was typical.

"What, again?"

"Dad, come off it. She didn't 'try to kill herself.' She killed herself. Period. End. Do you get it or do I have to start over?"

Silence. Was he taking it in or waiting for more information? For a split second, a neon sign paraded through Jaime's head, bearing the phrase from *Tango Varsoviano*: "shut up, che, shut up," spoken to an imaginary listener by a woman so different and yet so similar to his own.

"Are you sure, Lucas?"

"I'm not an idi . . ."

"I didn't mean that. What I'm asking is could it have been a heart attack, a stroke? How do you know she killed herself? What did you find?"

Lucas stifled a snort of impatience. His father never accepted any information without asking a thousand questions, only to go over the entire repertoire all over again, and even then, continue to have doubts as to whether things really were the way they were.

"I didn't find anything. I didn't look either. I know she killed herself. I want you to come. Someone has to deal with this."

He'd said it again. Mom had become, from that moment on, a "this:" a body to be disposed of, a tedious process, an obituary in the newspaper . . . this.

"I'm on my way. But please, in the meantime, look around."

Jaime hung up first. That was new. Usually with him the goodbyes took forever. Mom used to say he was incapable of saying goodbye, of placing that final period, changing the channel when he didn't like the show he was watching. Well, that was one problem she didn't have. She faced everything with the final period at the beginning. Case in point. Dad was more than mistaken in thinking that he was going to start looking around . . . for what? There was no blood. "Messy" deaths, as she called them, gave Mom the chills—as in those involving guns, knives, heights. Besides, in Lucas' mind, to paraphrase a title from Cortázar, whose work he actually was very familiar with when he wasn't trying to annoy Mom, the bedroom was "a room taken." He estimated that it would take Jaime about an hour to get there and had the impulse to call Estela. He started to dial, but by the second digit had thought better of it. She would run to console him, but he wasn't sure he needed consolation. He was boiling with anger, that was for sure, and he also could sense a glimmer of relief he found incomprehensible.

He passed the time checking his e-mail—nothing interesting—and put on a kettle to boil for coffee. Dad operated on coffee and cigarettes, Mom on alcohol and cigarettes, tranquilizers and cigarettes and, in her best moments, just cigarettes. Maybe that's why the thing about the heart attack had occurred to Dad? What lack of intuition, my God. My God. What God? Under the icon of which God were they going to bury her? Once, a long time ago, when Lucas wasn't even a fantasy in the mind of the adolescent Sylvia, she had tried—always trying, Mom—to follow the God of her origins, the God of Israel. Lucas had no idea when and why she had become an atheist. When she'd had him, not only had she allowed, she'd encouraged his baptism in the Catholic faith of his father's family. Yet throughout his childhood, she had fueled his imagination with stories of the people of Israel, and she'd pounded it into his head that Christianity had come *after* Christ, since Jesus was born, lived, and died a Jew. Christianity was the continuity while Judaism was the holding fast, the waiting until the end of time, but they were joined like arm and hand, stem and glass. However, when in his first awareness of death he'd tortured her with questions about eternal life, the beyond, the soul, she would respond, "If you believe, then it exists. But I don't believe in it."

And he had despaired. He could not comprehend the logic of "it exists if you believe it." He needed a concrete statement, a yes or a no. How were things to exist for him, when, for Mom, they did not?

As he prepared the tray and cups a faint, very faint stab of remorse made his hands tremble. Mom often had wanted to tell him about herself, about that other person she'd been before she was his mom, but he would get impatient. It wasn't the same as when she told stories she or Dad had made up. He never tired of hearing those. Mom's real life had to be incredibly boring. He repeated to himself in a hoarse murmur, "I didn't know her." He also decided that she should have insisted; in the end, she was the adult and he the child. But she would just fall into silence and he'd go play war with Dad.

Jaime found him sitting in the kitchen, with a lost, inward expression. Though he had house keys, since Sylvia had never asked for them or changed the locks, he had always felt it appropriate to ring the door bell if he needed to come in. It had happened a couple of times early in the separation. Clothes or papers he had not taken with him carried him back to a place that in a way still seemed like his own and yet strange at the same time. Today was special. He was about to ring the doorbell when he changed his mind and cautiously used the keys, so as not to wake Sylvia. He realized the enormity of the lapse only when faced with the specter of Lucas, an angular silhouette chiseled against the polished white of the refrigerator.

They embraced tightly, for a long while, until Lucas freed himself and served the coffee. Jaime made no effort to drink it right away. He was putting it off. And Lucas did not rush him. There was no one around to tell them off for being late anymore.

He was the one who had gotten there late. If he'd returned earlier . . . but how much earlier? It was just occurring to him that he hadn't considered the time or day she died. His rejection of the very notion of it was such that, despite having watched countless movies and police shows, he had paid no attention to the specifics. He did not know if those livid spots he had noticed always appeared and, if so, how many hours after death. But he did recall having heard of rigor mortis and how it wore off after x number of hours. When he'd shaken her, Mom's body had been as flexible as rubber, in other words, she'd been dead a long time . . . or maybe she'd only just died? He wouldn't know for sure unless he went back to check . . . him or someone. Dad. Or a doctor? Shouldn't they call a doctor to certify all of this? And the doctor, wouldn't he tell them to call the police? Oh, Mom, you made it pretty complicated for us. You didn't care about any of it.

Jaime was reading his train of thought in his eyes, because both of their thoughts were heading down the same track. Both could hear the monotonous litany that Sylvia had repeated during her second, and worst, bout of depression: "I'm the idiot who deals with all the problems. When I'm dead, you're going to have to take care of it all by yourselves."

Twirling the empty cup around on the plate, he felt that this—in a different sense from Lucas' "this"—was unfair. Both of them, father and son, had taken care of things as far as best they could, considering the difficulties of living with a wife and mother consumed by bitterness, wallowing in sadness, gone the spark of interest toward herself and others. The truth was that over the years, they had opted to escape from Sylvia, overwhelmed by her merciless attacks, sometimes translated into a desperate silence and at others a verbal violence that cut them to the quick, leaving them with an infinite number of questions she'd refuse to answer and that he, it was true, had not mentioned to the successive psychiatrists.

Besides, they had not expressed a need to talk with him and he didn't really understand such matters anyway. There had been years and years of fierce battles. Sylvia didn't play war, she waged war, and she took hostages. He supposed she had won. A Pyrrhic victory for him, who appreciated life. And her life? Sylvia always insisted that her life was a grotesque imitation, the life of an automaton, operated by a feeble mechanism that compelled her to don the mask of a functional person Monday through Friday, from 8 a.m. to 10 p.m. and when the cord ran out, pushed her onto the bed for the rest of the time.

While he was still living in the house, and even after he'd stopped worrying about her, he made sure she ate with a certain regularity. But Sylvia never ate lunch and she had dinner in bed, where she had sequestered all of her things: the cigarettes—which he bought because she didn't even do that for herself—the agenda, pen, the glass of wine, the innumerable medicine containers, Plafi. The little bear nestled on her breast received the only expressions of tenderness Sylvia was capable of by that time. If Jaime made as if to touch her, she would recoil as if from some sort of filthy vermin, always with the same refrain NO—NOT YOU. In the end, Jaime was careful to avoid even brushing against her.

Sometimes the teenaged Lucas would stretch out next to his mother when he still didn't have his own television. But mainly he avoided her or she would get exasperated without his knowing why and would send him from the room, slamming the door and forbidding him to return.

Jaime knew very little about how life had transpired between mother and son after his departure, but he remembered how it had been all those years before her sickness. God, she wasn't the same person. Which God? Father, Son and Holy Spirit, receive her immortal soul and forgive her sin—unforgivable—of rejecting Your most precious gift. If she had actually taken her own life, that is. It was necessary to go into the bedroom.

He could tell from Lucas' face that he would have to do it on his own. He stood, stroked his head. He thought he detected a slight motion of rebuff.

It wasn't easy for Jaime to return to the room where he hadn't set foot for years. For a long time, it had been the center of his universe. Early in his marriage, he had worked in a suburban bank and, returning downtown, the miles would fly by as he thought of Sylvia, with the table set and dinner ready, all delicious new dishes. She hated serving the same menu twice. But she wasn't waiting for him tired, or bustling about in the kitchen, but rather seated on the bed, perfectly composed, her head reclining against the colonial style headboard, long legs on the bedcover, hugging a pillow that concealed her chest and part of her face. Her nose would emerge, and her black shining eyes, the thick brows delicately arched, and he would kiss her and hug her just like that, pillow and all, because in reality it wasn't just any pillow: it was Baby Bear. They had created the bear family in their own couple fantasy: he was the Bear, or Papa Bear, or Dr. Bear, and she was "Osi" the little bear or little she-bear. Almost immediately, "Osezno" the bear cub appeared, Osi's baby brother. Perpetually cold, she was able to warm up in his arms. "My little oven," she called him. And he felt as if he could do anything: he was young, good-looking, a budding professional, and he loved her for being sweet, beautiful, spoiled, intelligent, for being Sylvia. He wanted to protect her, take care of her, and she would laugh an open, happy laugh. She was strong and solid, lover and accomplice, his wife, future mother of the children they would have when he was a little farther along in his career and she could stay home more.

Before coming to a stop on her body, his eyes traveled over the walls, the windows, the furniture. It was hard for him to believe that Sylvia hadn't changed a thing. The paint, stained on the walls and peeling off the ceiling, was the same as when he had painted the entire house, as an offering, before he left. The furniture, now in a state of absolute disrepair, had inaugurated their lives together. In their plans for purchases and progress, Sylvia would laugh: "this bed stays. I'm never going to want another one."

And there it was, the tracery broken and the frame chipped. And Sylvia lay atop it, on the left side—her side. It suddenly occurred to him that the other side, the one he'd left vacant, probably had remained so these six years, as if it were one of his belongings that he would come for one day and carry off in a suitcase.

He stopped deluding himself with the illusion of a natural death. Lucas was right. It was suicide. One didn't need a doctor to see that. Sobs choked him. He lay down beside her, took her hands—she couldn't rebuff him now—and began to speak softly, in broken phrases, convinced with all his heart that her soul remained nearby ("if you believe, it exists") waiting for him, calling him.

NO—NOT YOU

"And who, if not me?" he would answer at first, when he took it as just another game. But now the truth was, who else besides him?

"You're little, my love, so little. You dressed up like a big lady. You fooled them all, but I knew. We kept our secret, you and me . . . that you were a little bear—'Osi'. You see osis can't live in the human world because their little osi fur and their little osi souls get hurt. And osis can't live in solitude, Sylvita. When you were bad off you'd say you were a very lonely bear, that you had been on your own since you were born and it would always be like that. Love didn't reach you. Remember when you turned yourself into a duck that lived in a nest surrounded by thorns so the other little animals wouldn't get in? Why did you work so hard to erect your solitude? Why, all of a sudden, did you begin to die? I know you wanted things I didn't give you, that I couldn't give you, but remember, you said you didn't want anything, that nothing made you happy. You wanted death to come to you and since it didn't you went looking for it; you insisted. You brought it on. Well, I've already lost so much, what's one more scar? But your son? You used to say, when you fell into that well of insanity, 'He's grown, I educated him. He doesn't need me anymore, except to pay his bills, just like you.' And when you had those horrible attacks of hate, and you called him 'that fucking boy'—you didn't believe we loved you. If you believe, it exists, remember? What did you believe in? In pain, in the intolerable agony of pretending to be someone else on the outside while you were in pieces inside, in death as part of the solution. You created a disaster. Because you made a choice. You didn't have the right, Sylvia. Remember how you used to say you had the world at your feet, until the world kicked your feet out from under you. You did it again. I don't know how much the world really cares, but Lucky will be thinking, 'Given the choice of being my mother or dying, she preferred to die.' You were moved by such distant beings: remember how you cried over the documentaries on the Gulf War? Lucky always complained that you were unpredictable, swinging from affection to disapproval, and then to utter indifference. I chanced to glimpse it and I was horrified. But you were no longer speaking to me, wouldn't answer me; you were already leaving."

Jaime's voice gradually trailed off. The rest, not much, was pronounced only in his mind. It was "what a shame, so much damage" and an Our Father for Sylvia and for them.

Then he released her hands.

Methodically, he began to search. Before calling the doctor, he hoped to find two things.

Chapter II

THE SEARCH

"Will it take much longer, Dad?"

Lucas wondered why his father was taking forever in the bedroom. Probably because he took forever in everything.

"He can't say goodbye to Mom," he thought. He asked so much of her, and she gave it to him I suppose. But did she give him what he was really asking for? Did they ever really understand each other?

He flinched as if to break off a train of thought dangerously reminiscent of Mom's ominous progressions.

Jaime's voice reached him through the closed door, grim and subdued.

"I asked you to look. You didn't. I'm not sure how long it will take."

Dad was getting angry. Him, he definitely knew well. The worst thing was when he started acting weird: a sure sign things weren't going well. Gnawing on his words, keeping his voice controlled and neutral, an embryonic anger, followed—or not—by an explosion of physical violence against some object. A kitchen tile split in two by the knife-edge of Dad's hand, before Lucas was born. He'd had an unpleasant scene with his boss and, since he couldn't split his head in two, he'd taken it out on the tile. The window in the maid's room dislocated from its frame for months. That time the argument had been with Mom.

Leave him be to look for whatever it was. In general, Lucas wasn't into assisting with the practicalities. He simply got out of the way until someone else had taken care of them. And with "that" in there, Dad was on his own. It was no secret how issues connected to death affected him. He went to his room to fool around on the computer. The upshot was that Mom had gone even farther away, without letting them know.

Jaime searched the drawers of both night tables. Some contained only dust and fuzz, while in others, an endless assortment of unrelated objects was interspersed with yellowed papers: supermarket receipts, Christmas cards, a blue notepad covered with enigmatic annotations ("Call M. . . . ," "232 X 8 ="). Why had Sylvia kept all of these things? Stupid question. She wasn't keeping them, she threw them away, anywhere. Anything that hid the trash from view was a garbage can. In one pile was an acrylic box with an emblem and the medal commemorating Lucas' elementary school graduation. Something shone behind the tarnished silver. Jaime removed the medal and found Sylvia's wedding ring. His eyes filled with tears. So some symbols were important to her. She had preserved them, in her own way. Perhaps they accompanied her in her crises or evoked times when she had (felt? believed she was?) happy.

Hair clips, handkerchiefs, stockings, safety pins. No trace of what he was looking for, and nothing on the closet shelves either. He emptied out pockets and purses: coins, pens, keys, bus tickets, lighters, which she was constantly losing and he buying her new ones. She'd lose them whenever she changed her purse and had ended up with a collection.

He was running out of possible places. But both things had to be there.

He felt underneath the pillows. Sylvia had a habit of hiding money in the pillowcases, along with those awful things she wrote, directed at no one in particular, each word a small scrap of suffering steeped in infinite pain. He could understand the words, but he knew only she could measure the pain. He'd read them furtively while she was in the bathroom vomiting bile every morning, then return them to their hiding places and act oblivious. What could he say to her? Her writings evoked a dimension that was completely unfathomable to him. Yes, he too felt hurt, sad, or depressed, but it was different. He was a man, a body and a mind and everything the combination was capable of producing, both good and bad. She, in those states, was a suppurating wound severed from anything he understood as human. An open sore, ungrounded, borderless, spreading towards death, always towards death. His hand traveled over some rectangular forms. There were the two boxes of pills, carefully resealed, the contents in Sylvia's system. She'd had time to do all of this . . . with what going on in her mind? And why did it torture him so much not to know how she'd spent those final moments? He'd mourned other deaths—his father, cancer, his mother, old age—in the same state of ignorance and yet, standing before Sylvia dead, the question was raised only by, only for, her.

Little by little, spasmodically squeezing the fatal little boxes, he realized that the scene itself answered his question. Scene—scenario: everything in sight had been cleaned and straightened up. Sylvia had gotten ready for bed, Plafi at her side, her being-not-being with whom she communicated, or *to* whom she communicated to the extent that she wasn't expecting or looking for reciprocity.

Plafi had been struck dumb when Sylvia's rejection of Lucas had erupted more frequently. Up to then, Lucas had lent him a mischievous and childish voice that had spun sequences of infinite tenderness.

Always initiated by the baby bear, these were three-way exchanges between the mother, Plafi, and the voice of Lucas, from which Jaime was excluded. Creeping along Sylvia's stomach held between Lucky's two fingers, an insatiable Plafi begged:

"Mommy, mommy, give me some cash."

"And why would a baby bear need cash?" She'd enter into the game, over and over again a thousand times with no variation.

"To buy little hats."

"But you already have lots of little hats!"

"Yes, but I saw a more expensive one. I want the more expensive one! I am a first class baby bear! I have to have an ACME hat! And I also want more expensive pencils, and more expensive toy cars, and . . ."

"If you didn't spend your money you might . . ."

"No! Cash is for spending. If you don't give me cash I'll hold a sit-down strike!"

"What do you mean a sit-down strike?"

"Like this!" and Lucky would sit Plafi on top of Sylvia's stomach and make him jump up and down. "A sit-down strike in protest! Like on TV!"

"Hmm . . . too much TV it seems to me."

"I'll go with Tadam Huteim! He'll definitely give me some cash for the most expensive guns. Tadam Huteim! Tadam Huteim!"

Yelling and jumping up and down, Plafi would vanish in a huff, only to shyly poke out his ears and ask:

"Are you mad, Mommy?"

No, that didn't make her mad. She enjoyed it, and Jaime, the witness to such dialogues, wondered to what extent Lucky expressed himself through Plafi. He also was vaguely intrigued by the need for a third party: between himself and Sylvia it was Osezno the bear cub, between Sylvia and Lucky, Plafito. Was it that she couldn't manage without a buffer? Or that they didn't dare approach her without a "shield?"

Plafi's presence on the pillow struck him as sinister. The stuffed toy and the bear cub had denoted a "that's as close as you get, no closer." It was impossible to reach her except through fantasy, even in those rare moments when her attention seemed distracted from her inanimate protectors. Jaime sighed, saying once again,

"You fooled them all, but I knew."

And almost without realizing it, just to know, he tossed aside the carefully folded nightshirt.

Pages from a small blue notebook slid to the floor.

There it was.

The nightshirt was concealing her real nakedness: the word.

Jaime did not want to see, much less read, the pinched handwriting, clear and legible in form but explosive in meanings he could never quite put together. Sylvia was right, he talked even out the elbows, but she got even on paper and he found it impossible to recognize himself in the faces of the monster whose profile was traced in line after line. He was a man, body, mind. . . .

Sylvia's body was superfluous to her. It was a bothersome charge she had to feed, dress, wash, move around, an unpleasant impediment that she mistreated in every way possible. To expose it or cover it was all the same to her: she wasn't a body, she'd say; she didn't even have a body. Jaime would make her buy clothes, with the excuse of what her clients, or her colleagues, or her friends would say. He complimented her on her figure. At 50 she still had the body of a girl. She was indifferent to all of it. She'd just turn to him with her hard, icy stare, informing him that her figure was merely a product of chance and dressing it, or brushing a comb through her hair, were merely awkward concessions to those who judged others by their appearance. She walked past mirrors without a pause and Jaime had begun to think that, in revenge, the mirrors refused to reflect her. Ironically, her body demanded her attention through a thousand contrivances and she, writhing in pain, fought back. "If you don't believe, it doesn't exist." The body withdrew, defeated, leaving behind the counterpoint to pain: zero pleasure. NO—NOT YOU.

"Come on, Dad!" Is there a lot left to do?"

Jaime did not answer. But yes, there was a lot left: Sylvia was gone for the rest of their lives.

He gathered the pages, sat down on his side of the bed, and began to read.

Chapter III

THE LETTER

"I have nothing to say to anyone in particular. I don't think I owe any explanations. I am exercising my right to decide how much is enough. I can imagine it as if I were there watching: Lucas indignant, and his father, miracle of miracles, speechless.

Know that you are strangers. If it is easier for you, believe that I once loved you. Do not feel guilty about my death. It is mine—death, not guilt—and I take sole responsibility for it. It could have been different had I been different. Different from myself, because I am very different from you, as if I were a Martian. I am not going to talk about the past. Life was an experience I would have preferred to miss. No one asked me whether I wanted to live it or not. I endured it. The only thing that made it tolerable at times was the certainty that it would end. I was never afraid of my own death; life terrified me. 'Tomorrow' was the sinister word that evoked today's anguish and yesterday's, and the eternity that went before. 'Afterward,' 'later on,' were synonymous with the suffering still to come.

It is over. I will not be part of any more tomorrows.

I am sorry that for Lucas and Jaime I am going to become a yesterday; how I wish memory could be erased, or changed to a different, happier one. One day (right Lucas?) memories will be custom made for the one doing the remembering.

I have to ask you—and I am sorry for this too, but there are no substitutes for the rituals of death—that there be no speeches or wakes or tears from those who go to view the dead and cry about something else. I do not want any hypocrites lamenting the "terrible loss"... Closed casket and cremation.

Just toss the ashes.

I do not care what you do with my things, although it would be better not to keep them. If you do it will be harder to forget. I DO NOT want my books and papers to remain after I am gone. I do not want them to be given to friends or strangers, and I do not want you to save them either. When Lucas was little, he loved to make bonfires with whatever he had on hand. Well, this is his big chance.

I, who was nothing, do not wish to leave anything behind. And yet Lucas remains. But he is not mine. I gave him life. Maybe it was a mistake, a contradiction that life could be born from nothing. I do not fully understand how I could have let it happen. He is so unlike me that I am surprised he is my son. His good fortune.

Breathe, both of you. Think, simply, that Sylvia has removed the problem of Sylvia from your shoulders. I am not saying I did it for you. I did it for me. I am selfish, as you know. It is no tragedy either. I could have died of any disease, in an accident, or a plane crash. But no. I died of death."

Sylvia

Jaime deposited the pages on the bed. His hands were shaking. Lucas shouldn't read this letter. And yet indirectly it was addressed to him, even though she'd said it wasn't for anyone. *"Know that you are strangers."* Were there no limits to her cruelty? The ex husband could come to accept himself as a stranger. The son had been, moreover, a mistake?

Images from their first years of marriage obscured the grimy walls. He had wanted children, several. He'd felt secure in this banking career and it was time. All of a sudden, she'd want triplets, or three sons in a row, yet she kept taking the pill. Both of their families were keeping an expectant eye on them. The "so when will it be?" hung in the air.

Sylvia did not want children.

At thirty, with eight years in the legal field on top of a childhood and adolescence devoid of love, she intuited that she was not capable of being a good mother. She believed she loved Jaime, but she also said, "you learn to love by being loved when you're young." Ever since she could remember, she had felt like a bother, a little creature with huge questioning eyes, the object of her mother's highest praise, "She's a little doll. She stays wherever you put her."

Getting married had also not been part of her plans. Her favorite joke was that Jaime, "had caught her unawares" when she said yes. Perhaps drawn along by the need for love, she'd convinced herself that Jaime's love for her would replace the love she'd never received even when, convulsed with tears, she'd begged her father, then her mother: "Love me!" They had regarded her uncomprehendingly. They took care of her, fed her, educated her. Her father, especially, took her out and gave her pretty toys, the best of all being Simon bear, with which the child never parted except to go to school. What did she want? What did those outbursts of abandonment mean? Her mother, impatient, reacted in a pragmatic, effective manner: "Enough of that idiocy or I'll lock you in your room until you're finished with your tantrum." Her father, a mild-mannered, unhurried man, would pull her onto his lap and ask: "Now then, Sylvita, tell me what is going on." And she went from "love me" to an enigmatic phrase that would become a refrain throughout her childhood. "I want something that is something but isn't anything."

When Jaime had confronted her directly with the question, "Are we going to have a baby or not?" she'd hidden behind the why bring innocents into this fucked up world that was only going to keep getting more hostile. It wasn't just an excuse: she genuinely felt in her bones that if hell existed, it was most certainly located on Earth. But the underlying reason had to do with her virtual certainty that she, who was not endowed with the ability to love, would be unable to give it to her children. The same wounds would therefore be inflicted on them, and so the cycle could continue *ad infinitum*.

Jaime had insisted and she'd eventually come to accept that everyone is blessed, even if ever so fleetingly, with the ability to give and receive love. How could she not love that little speck of the two of them? How could she not be loved by a child who is conceived in love?

The pregnancy proceeded under this illusion. They were the only nine months of her adult life free from nausea and vomiting. But when she gave birth and her fantasies about motherhood were replaced by a baby made of flesh and bones, so fragile, whom she felt powerless to shield with an elusive love she'd never been able to snare or be ensnared by, she knew there would be no others. And this only child, Lucas, should have to endure the insult of being called a stranger, added to the injury of the corpse left behind so that he, and only he, should find it? It didn't seem fair to Jaime, but he was also incapable of making a decision about it. Among the mass of contradictions knotting the tortuous path of the labyrinth, she had devoted herself to law to be "a soldier of justice." And yet, when it didn't have to do with her clients, she'd explored every possible form of arbitrariness based on her "I hate," which invoked a particular version of "I accuse."

Finally—as usual—he opted for the path of least resistance. He took the letter, closed the door, and returned to the kitchen.

Lucas had not moved, frozen in who knew what memories, what thoughts.

"I found a letter," announced the father. "I don't know if you want to read it."

Lucas held out his hand for it, absorbing the contents without lingering on the words.

"She was right," he murmured. "I don't know her, but I recognize her. I was always a stranger to her, and she to me."

He began to crumble it up to toss it in the trash, but Jaime stopped him.

"No! It's documentation! It's going to save us a lot of paperwork. And it's also a sort of last will. It asks us to do things. I think we owe it to her."

Lucas handed him the page without looking at him. In order to avoid any so-called "paperwork," his father had allowed any difficulties involving papers, negotiations with creditors and debtors, or even simple claims, to reach extremes beyond the point of no return. In a word, he just let them lie, accumulating lawsuits against him that went crashing smack into nothing, because he wouldn't show up when he was supposed to either. While it was true he had no money to pay for legal representation, the simple fact was that none of it concerned him. The country, the bad governments, were to blame for the stranglehold placed on small business, a sector he had joined when the bank where he was working had taken a substantial number of high-level staff members off its hands by tempting them with voluntary retirement.

He was in debt to God and the Virgin Mary. According to Lucas' figures, several lifetimes wouldn't be enough to pay it all off, yet the debt to Sylvia, the fulfillment of those wishes intended to erase every trace of her existence, that one he felt obligated to pay.

Lucas had not decided whether he was going to allow it.

Who was she to give orders when she hadn't even bothered to destroy the objects in question before leaving?

The dead are dead. Lucas didn't believe in all that stuff about carrying out posthumous wishes, much less when they were merely strangers to her. True as it might have been, the word cut like the crudest of insults. He shoved the thought aside as if it were a physical act in order to concentrate on the requests. No announcement meant inventing a thousand and one explanations for whoever might call on the phone or ask after his mother during some chance encounter or social occasion. Not to mention the clients who surely were left adrift in the few or many cases she would have been handling. Imaginary—sickening—conversations told him that having to answer the same questions over and over again was just one more punishment Sylvia had heaped on him. She who abhorred blows, had been a master of psychological torture.

A conversation bordering on the grotesque began to take shape in his ears.

"Lucas, it's Clara, may I speak with your mother?

"My mother died last week."

"What! Oh God, what happened?"

Well, he could offer any number of versions. She was run over by a bus. She'd slipped in the shower and cracked her head on the marble corner. She'd choked on a fish bone. It was all possible. It was all believable.

"She committed suicide."

"She couldn't have! Why the last time I saw her, on Tuesday, no, it was Wednesday, she was doing great. . . . We started to flesh out a project that . . ."

"It was on Sunday."

"But why didn't you tell me? This is horrible!"

"She didn't want us to tell anybody."

"But I'm . . . her best friend! Didn't it occur to you that 'anybody' meant other people?"

Each person who heard the news was going to react in the same way. Each would feel that he or she was not included in the absolute "anybody" with which Sylvia rid herself of those who, in their own way, in whatever way she would have allowed it, had accompanied her for shorter or longer periods of time.

Lucas did not want to go through all that on the telephone, in the street, in public places, or in private. The death would be announced. The rest . . . he could discuss with his father. Jaime tried to talk him out of it. He trotted out the practical aspect: funeral announcements cost money. He could not afford it.

"Don't worry about it, Dad. She always had a little something put aside 'just in case'."

"But not for something like this! If it says, specifically . . ."

"I don't give a shit what it says. Call the doctor. And then La Nación. It's the one the people who need to know read."

"The doctor? The psychiatrist, or an internist?" Jaime realized that in her utter rejection of her body, Sylvia probably didn't have an internist. The only two times he could recall her going to a doctor had been imposed on her by the excruciating pain of a biliary colic the first time, and years later by an intestinal infection that had left her too weak to keep refusing. Which was not to say there weren't other episodes that had required medical attention. In at least one instance, Sylvia had risked her life by ignoring it because it easily could have been cancer. She'd just let it go. What did she care about life?

Lucas also had no idea whether she'd had a more or less regular relationship with any internist. On the other hand, the psychiatrist was, of course, a doctor and would know what to do. Jaime returned to the bedroom to retrieve the agenda Sylvia usually carried in whichever purse she happened to be using. When he'd dumped everything out in search of the letter, he had done it mechanically, without paying attention. Opening the door of the closet where Sylvia kept her purses he paused for a minute, perplexed by the amorphous pile of different colors, sizes, and shapes. Which one could it be? Reaching for the one on top, he was assailed by the feeling that for the second time in half an hour, he was engaged in something forbidden: Sylvia hated it when they mixed up her purses. She wouldn't reproach him now, yet in a way the stiff body constituted itself into one long chain of reproaches, for the past, the present, and for what was still to come. He forced himself to open the clasp and by sheer luck the agenda was right there in plain view. Jaime closed the closet door and went over to the telephone in the living room. But he did not place the call; not yet. First he sat down on the leather sofa, whose back and armrests had suffered a furious attack with a pair of scissors on one of those Sundays when he and Lucas were enjoying a day at the club. He had insisted it should be reupholstered, but Sylvia would not hear of it.

"Leave it as it is. It will serve as a reminder, to all of us."

To her, to throw kindling on new avenues of fury. To them, so they would keep in mind what she was capable of. Jaime wondered why she had let herself sink into irrationality. He knew for certain that when Sylvia was out of control he was consumed by terror. He imagined her capable even of murder. For a time, he had hidden two sharp kitchen knives because he could imagine being stabbed in the defenseless sleep of which Sylvia was so bitterly envious. On the days when, fed up with the disorder in the form of clothing, papers, and old periodicals strewn about the house—the joint masterpiece of father and son—she would threaten to take care of it once and for all "by setting fire to the whole thing," he would break into a cold sweat during nightmares in which the flames tortured their bodies and reduced the offending articles to unrecognizable lumps. He never spoke of it to her. To do so would have been tantamount to acknowledging the power of her insanity, leaving himself naked, exposed, defenseless. But she, his Sylvia, wasn't like that! Yet she was, and she was also the other, and perhaps how many others? He left a brief message on the psychiatrist's cell phone.

Dr. Garnet did not usually turn on his cell on weekends, unless he was involved in a serious case. It was his wife who motioned to him that it was vibrating and practically insisted he check to see what it was about. He returned the call right away with a curt, "I'm on my way," and no further question or comment.

Heading downtown from his luxurious home in Martínez, he went over the Sylvia case in his mind, since he would not have time to stop by the office to pick up his notes. He would do it later and possibly use them to present a paper at the next conference. He wondered fleetingly why he hadn't seen it coming, but discarded the notion almost violently. He wasn't a magician and she had deceived him. One way or another, patients always lie whether they know it or not, and they always hide things, even when they don't intend to. Garnet intuited that this act was not the result of a sudden impulse, but rather had been carefully planned and that, in a way, she had used him, sometimes as a pawn and sometimes as a king, in a game of chess. As a pawn he was disposable and to top it off, she had checkmated him. She had shut down all movement with no warning, sending up smoke screens that had kept him from seeing what she was up to. And now, she had wiped him off the board. Looking for a parking spot, he was frankly angry. The suicide of a patient whom he had diagnosed as non-suicidal could damage his professional reputation. Not to mention that the family could lay the blame on him publicly as well as privately.

This . . . "lady" had been a hard nut to crack from the start.

During their initial interviews she had described her previous therapeutic experiences, of which only one, the first, appeared to have been relatively successful. When she was nineteen years old, torn between loyalty to her mother, whom she claimed not to love but to whom she owed her upbringing and education, and her weakness for her father—instilled in her by his own weakness in facing up to life—she had consulted an eminent psychoanalyst recommended to her by an older friend. After listening to the reasons for her visit and asking a few questions, the now deceased Dr. Estrada had refused to psychoanalyze her, saying it was not a good idea to tear down a whole building just because of a few problem areas. He offered her a brief period of support therapy from which she had gleaned two messages she would recall throughout her life: "if you try to live your mother's life, or your father's, you will end up living neither theirs nor your own," and "there are never just two paths, you have to find a third."

From the other treatments she had retained little more than a shrug toward the various specialists: good or bad, they hadn't helped her.

As he waited for someone to answer the door, he decided that Sylvia had attached her own particular reading to those golden words. She hadn't lived her parents' life, nor had she lived her own and the truth was, she'd chosen a third path to the extent that the other two, an intolerable life or trying to change life, had not interested her enough to keep on struggling.

After a firm handshake, a shaken and wordless Jaime guided him into the apartment. Garnet preferred to ask a couple of questions before seeing his—patient? Seated in the living room, the place elicited in him a strong feeling of distaste combined with some surprise: dust and dirt everywhere. Sylvia had never mentioned this to him and it wasn't easy to guess judging from her less than attractive, yet meticulously neat appearance. The responses he obtained shed no light on anything out of the ordinary that might have occurred before the suicide. Friday evening and the weekend were an unknown quantity, although deep down he no longer believed they were relevant. To the contrary, he was inclined to believe the decision had been made long ago and weighed at length. It had only remained to select the moment, all the while keeping him entertained, successfully, expatiating about future plans, day to day activities, with ups and downs but seemingly ensconced in life, speaking from the standpoint of life.

What struck him was that neither the ex husband nor the son had turned to him for explanations. In some visceral way he understood why they were not getting him involved. This left him even more left out than what she had done to him by hiding what she was up to. He was irritated and put out, but this was not the moment to reflect on his own role in a denouement he would call absurd. He refused to intervene as a physician and suggested a clinician be called. At their perplexed looks—Sylvia had frequented none—he suggested an emergency physician. They told him they'd think about it and saw him out with a mixture of courtesy and absence that made him feel even worse. He did not offer his condolences as he left. Sylvia had splintered off into a body to be disposed of by others, while the case of Sylvia would bear juicy fruit in the discussion forums in which he took part.

For Lucas, practically in an instant—oh sacrilege, an assault on that realm of knowledge where stacks upon stacks of Garnets disputed the throne—his mother's psychiatrist left off being "the competent professional" and passed over to the category of idiot. And one doesn't ask questions of an idiot, because his responses will be idiotic. Lucas could not accept that there wasn't a real reason for the suicide. Ever since he'd learned the expression, he had bombarded his parents for the real reason for one thing or another, flying into a tantrum when Jaime would say teasingly, "Has someone ever, even once, seen the real reason for something?" Sylvia made a bit more of an effort to explain to him that truths were relative and partial, and reasons subjective. Even so, there had to be a reason. He'd be satisfied with just knowing what it was, even if he didn't understand it.

As she prepared the scene of her death, Sylvia had never stopped asking herself the real reason. She could list so many, and they all sounded empty. Others had gone through situations infinitely more painful, been subjected to unimaginable horrors, and yet held on to the spark of life, sustained by the hope of a miracle that would fan it into a blaze. The survivors. What a terrifying word: *super vivere*. How ironic the allusion to hovering above life when in reality what it named was infrahuman. Ultimately she decided the question would have to be posed by the rest of them, by those she was electing to abandon, those from whom she had wished to extricate herself. Surely they would find some answer that would satisfy them, or not, but she would not be there to hear the speculations, the explanations, the imprecations. That was the whole point. To not be there. She'd been putting it off—she who hated procrastination—hoping against hope it would be possible for her to change something until, on her own again that weekend, she had realized once and for all that nothing was ever going to change. Things were only going to get worse for her and for Lucas if she stayed . . . alive, so to speak. Sometimes she didn't love him, it was true. And yet sometimes she did love him and then she would encourage him not to love her. What you don't love you don't miss and you don't mourn. She was superfluous. She always had been superfluous in other people's lives.

"Ms. Meyer, thank you so much for what you have done. I'll never forget it."

"Never" was five minutes. The problem resolved, the fees paid, the majority of her clients, who called themselves her friends ("you have a true friend in me count on me for anything you need") would vanish forever. Or at least until the next legal difficulty.

Some of the more conscientious invited her to their children's weddings or to their own second or third weddings. At first, Sylvia had been naïve enough to show up. She desisted when she realized that they invited her in part out of obligation and in part to show her off as "Ms. Meyer, our attorney, the one who saved us from . . . , so horrible! Remember we were telling you about it?" Ultimately, it had to do with a product, not a relationship between people, and yet these were people she knew—thought she knew well—men and women whom she'd defended successfully, from the moment they'd come into her office overwhelmed by matters handled within and outside the codes, matters that would never have reached the boiling point had they been more prudent and consulted in time. From the far side of her desk they laid bare their miseries, their infidelities, the mistreatment to which they had been subjected or subjected others. They cried and yelled, threatened and cursed.

Sylvia knew everything there was to know about them. All they knew about her was that she had a well-deserved reputation as a brilliant lawyer. And what she displayed outwardly was the mask of her implacable self-assurance, her eternal calm. She could not allow herself to let on that they were equals. It simply wasn't good for business. Besides, they wouldn't have wanted to see the essence of the Sylvia she was during that period—or had always been? She'd created the perfect mask and even so, it never ceased to amaze her that none of her clients, or colleagues, or alleged friends had glimpsed the deep creases tearing at it barely a millimeter away from the perfectly composed facial muscles, the eyes trained to show interest, attention, dedication. She had no doubt that behind her back the criticism flew, but it took a different tack.

"She doesn't touch it unless it's all wrapped up," muttered a less successful lawyer.

"I can't understand how she hung on to that good-looking husband of hers all that time. And on top of that, she was the one who kicked him out," snorted another, whose relationships tended to be on the short side.

"Attractive she is not," commented the men clustered in the cafés adjacent to the Courts.

As she arranged herself on the bed and swallowed the pills five at a time, she was talking to herself, her smile traversed by tears.

"You're going to be all right now, Sylvita. Everything's going to be fine. You'll be able to sleep without anyone waking you up. It was lucky you found out through Estela about the surprise they were planning for Lucas: that year-long trip he really wanted to make, and surely wouldn't have, thinking about what might happen to you if he weren't there to take care of you. But he, poor guy, never really took care of you. Just as with love, you have to learn how to take care of someone.

And who taught him, us? Poor little Lucas; he inherited the worst of both of us. Indecision and blindness on Jaime's side, intransigence and all or nothing on mine. A marvelous combination when it comes to inspiring affection, or giving it. Nonetheless, Estela and her family love him. Like a stray cat taken in from the streets perhaps, but they love him. And now he's going to be able to take the trip without worrying that he has to come back out of some obligation to me. But it's not because of that, not that, it's for me, for me . . ." Her thoughts began to dissolve into unconnected words, and the one that persisted, even when her body, so often maligned, had nearly stopped responding, was "Sylvita," her word of love for some part of herself she had never been able to show and that Jaime had never been able to penetrate, not even when he'd tried so hard—confused by the farce she'd staged so everything would come out okay, so long as her determination to want to be "normal" had lasted—to show her that love was possible.

"Shall I call Emergencies?" Lucas wanted to get things moving so one way or another, they'd take that thing away.

But his father said, "no" with a firmness Lucas had never heard before.

"No," repeated Jaime. "There will be no police, no autopsy, no scandal. Leave it to me."

Lucas felt goose bumps rise on his skin. It was always dangerous to leave it to him. Experience had shown that when it was left up to Jaime everything turned out wrong. It was almost worse than when he did nothing. He was afraid to ask and deep down, he didn't really want to know anyway.

"I'm going out for a while. Don't answer the telephone."

"I have to talk to Estela at least."

"Later. And wait for me here"

"Alone with her? After the hours I had to stand it until you got here? While she rots? Don't you smell something already?"

"It smelled from the first moment. Odors. The smells of death. Be a man, all right?"

And the oak door marked for Lucas the extremes of his vigil, accompanying a mother who, were she able to speak, would certainly be telling him, *"leave me alone."*

Chapter IV

THE WAKE

The funeral parlor matched the truncated, badly paved streets of a nameless quarter reached from the highway by way of a narrow, unmarked side road. The place looked like an allegory for the mortal remains we become, and the bald, obese man seated behind the miserable desk knew perfectly well that, in death as in life, it is not good business to mix the social classes. It was no accident that, after a careful examination of the market, he had decided to target his supply to those of modest means. It was not a bad idea. On the one hand, the same lack of resources made them more vulnerable to disease which was bound to kill them sooner rather than later since, even when the public hospitals admitted them, the system always got them in the end: the bus fare each time they had an appointment, the missed hours during the endless waits—unpaid too, since they eked out a living with odd jobs—, the perpetual "come back tomorrow," or next week, or when the x-ray machine was fixed, or when a bed was available, or when the surgeon was on duty, or . . . They tended to be perseverant, yet sooner or later they gave up, whether out of exhaustion, desperation, or lack of funds. After a while it was hard to come up with the fare, lose a day's work, only to listen to some doctor dashing off a prescription and never even glancing up say, "you'll have to buy these medicines. Unfortunately I have no samples to give you." And even so, they continued down the road that ended at the funeral parlor. The bald, obese man knew how to wait, expertly administering a business that earned him considerable profits, because it never occurs to the poor to begrudge the dear departed a good burial. By whatever means, collection or loan, no corpse went without flowers or a handsome coffin—albeit of poor quality—, or a little room with their name rendered in plastic gold letters against a faux black velvet background. If there still wasn't enough money, the next of kin signed promissory notes, never even bringing up the price. They were too embarrassed to bargain over the cost of the trip to the Great Beyond and besides, others would do right by them when their time came. So the bald, obese man prospered, his generous soul deluged with blessings, utterly incapable of depriving the deceased of the final pleasure afforded by a dignified wake.

When Jaime's shadow slanted across the Formica desktop from behind which the bald, obese man had coaxed and defrauded so many tearful and confused relatives, the businessman could tell this tall, erect, self-possessed man did not fit in. But of course, he said to himself, what made me think he was a customer? And then he felt in his bones that something was very, very wrong. It must be something to do with the taxes, with the condition of the building, he'd be coming to complain . . . about what? He mopped at his damp forehead and smiled to himself. Who was going to complain about him, the benefactor of the poor? This job was really getting to him. A fleeting image of a little getaway to Brazil began to take shape in his mind, even as his common sense forced him to focus on the visitor, who was standing there in silence, waiting.

"Sir? May I help you?"

"Yes, I believe so." Without invitation, Jaime sat down and lit a cigarette. He braced himself firmly against the back of the uncomfortable plastic chair and crossed his legs.

The bald, obese man was becoming impatient. This man did not spill out his story like the others who could be neither restrained nor consoled. But of course, this was no customer. He'd have to draw him out, but carefully, making sure not to say anything that could be used against him later. Here we go again.

"Would you like to tell me what it relates to?"

Jaime inhaled deeply, releasing a cloud of smoke that enveloped his interlocutor, who experienced the fleeting optical illusion of having before him a faceless body. Out of the smoke, and only the smoke, the words reached him.

"I need a death certificate."

"Excuse me?" The bald, obese man was buying time to evaluate the request. It was not that he found the request disconcerting. There had been occasions when, in the case of deaths that were not quite as clear and always far from the eyes and ears of the police, he would turn to one of his well-established parallel activities: the provision of perfectly legitimate certificates signed by bona fide physicians who pocketed the fees no questions asked. This service was expensive and cash only, since it had to be divided between two, but since the rest could be paid on credit . . . Is there really anything the dear departed does not deserve, particularly if it can be solved with money?

But this man . . . he wasn't from the area. He did not mention a reference. He'd suspected that he was a tax assessor or something of the sort, but it could be much worse.

"I think there's been some sort of misunderstanding," he decided to begin with a friendly yet firm approach. You bring the certificate and the supporting documentation, and we take charge of the burial. Let me show you . . ."

Jaime interrupted him with a wave.

"You and I have both changed a lot. I was the son of the lathe operator on the corner," he gestured vaguely toward the right, "and we played ball with the neighborhood kids on the lot the next block over until the Yugoslavs came and built the factory and ran a barbed wire fence around the playing field." Changing to a more informal tone, he continued, "I took you home when the gang across the street beat you up, saying you were a fairy. You remember that? On my own, because the others shit in their pants and took off, without so much as opening their mouths. Your old man told me to ask for anything and he'd give it to me, because I'd saved his chubby little boy. I didn't want anything then. And your old man—a great guy your old man—he went on to his just reward. So now I'm coming to you."

And he tersely explained the whys and wherefores of his request, adding that he was still in touch with people who talked about the funeral business and how some of them operated in certain cases.

The bald, obese man forced himself to listen, but he was engulfed by powerful, buried images from his childhood that filled him with surprise and shame, and a sensation of never being able to escape the past.

The skinny, washed-out, freckle-faced boy, a terrible ball player who was only included in the games when there weren't enough players, who had helped him wordlessly, half carrying, half dragging him to his house, had become a gentleman. There was no trace whatsoever of the snot-nosed brat destined to become a lathe operator like his father and his grandfather before him.

As if reading his thoughts, Jaime remarked, "You don't look the worse for wear either. So, are you going to help me?"

"Yes, but it'll cost you. You have to think about what the doctor is risking, and myself, the company . . . I have a family, they . . ."

The familiar speech spilled out easily.

"I get it. Let's talk numbers. How much"

Well . . . for the certificate, 800 pesos. Then you have to select a casket, a room, the cemetery, and a bunch of other junk."

"Okay." He put Sylvia's paperwork on the table, sticking the money between the pages. "Go ahead with this part. The rest of it I'll have to discuss with my son."

The bald, obese man palmed the papers and the bills with one stubby, manicured hand.

"It'll be a few hours. Leave your number. I'll call you."

Back at the apartment, braced with a cup of coffee, he explained to Lucas what he'd done. Now they definitely had to get rid of the letter. They burned it together over the toilet and in one flush rid themselves of every last vestige of ash. Some of the charred words would burn in their minds for a long time—not the same ones for each of them. The associations and the questions, when recalled, would perhaps torment them. But that was another stage. *"For the time being, Sylvia, we're getting by just fine."*

"Pa, where did you get the cash?" It occurred to Lucky that it had been a while since his father had had 800 pesos in his pocket.

"It was some money given to me to pay for something. But since you said Mom had some savings . . . You can pay me back, I'll pay off what I was supposed to get, and whatever else comes up we'll pay with Mom's savings. Do you know where she kept them?"

No, Lucky didn't know. There was a checking account, usually empty because Sylvia withdrew the money as soon as her clients' checks cleared. Sometimes he saw her remove bills from the strangest places: CD cases, book covers, balled-up underwear. She always had the feeling she was missing cash.

"Lucky, haven't you seen some money that . . . ?"

"No, Ma, I haven't. Look again. Try to remember what you spent."

"But didn't I give you some to pay the phone bill?" You didn't bring me any change."

"That was last week, Ma. You said I should use what was left to get the oil changed."

These exchanges occurred on a daily basis with minor variations.

Sylvia had been a tightwad in the shared opinion of father and son. Depending on her mood, she'd give way too much without asking, or else refuse to pay the electricity bill.

"Let them cut it off. I don't give a damn."

Even she did not understand her peculiar relationship with money. She did know she was terrified of being without it. Many of her fantasies about "tomorrows" that tore her to pieces had to do with a day, it could be any day, in which, having lost her savings by giving in to Jaime's requests and unable to earn more money—for lack of clients, illness, insanity, for whatever reason—she would be reduced to begging.

"What exactly does 'begging' mean?" Garnet had asked her when she had brought up the word during a session to sum up one of those nights of tears and anguish.

"Begging is the height of indignity."

"Like when you feel as if Jaime is begging from you? So the flip side of begging is contempt toward the other person?"

Sylvia reflected for an instant. Yes, contempt was part of it. The fear of going from not being loved to being an object of contempt. And with that, she decided to keep her response to herself. At that moment she was not feeling up to tolerating the smile with which, she was sure, Garnet insinuated his own contempt. For Sylvia, begging took on corporal, hallucinatory forms: Sylvia in rags, squatting and shivering with a metal cup in hand on the front steps of a church. Sylvia wrapped in a blanket full of holes, reeking of vomit, her own and others', sleeping the sleep of cheap wine bought with the coins from the little cup. Sylvia beaten and kicked out of some space which, unbeknownst to her had been staked out by someone else invoking the "I got here first" rule. Sylvia in the act of begging, but unable to produce more than a gesture: the words would not come out of her mouth.

"We'll continue on Monday." Garnet walked her to the door and proposed they return to the subject next time. Something substantial had to emerge from this issue of indignity.

When the ghosts disappeared—which, one had to admit, wasn't very often—she gave. Deep inside herself she felt it wasn't so much giving as paying so that they would act out the farce that they loved her. And feeling it in her bones and soul, she rebelled against herself and against them. And she made them pay it back, with a lot of interest translated into apprehension: "what is she going to do now? What are we going to find?" The coin with so much value added relative to the mere money it represented.

Lucky, for once, gave in.

"We'll have to dig around for it. But I don't go into the bedroom, just so you know."

Between the kitchen pots and pans, freezer containers, laundry basket, and picture frames, father and son came up with seven thousand dollars. It occurred to Jaime that they were beggar's stashes. He also recalled, as a probable cause, the times that she'd put money away in one of the desk drawers and he'd announce: "Oh, I took out (a hundred, five hundred, two thousand) dollars. I'll pay you back next week."

Next week would collapse into another payment-debt discovered.

He had left, but she had persisted in defending herself . . . but from whom then?

Following a call from the bald, obese man, Bochi to his friends, the vehicle arrived to pick up the body.

Lucky shut himself in his room with the phone on his knees.

"You don't want to see her one last time? It will be a closed coffin you know."

It was the only concession to the deceased, since there would be notices and a wake.

But Lucky was already telling Estela everything, leaving his protagonist role abundantly clear.

She did not want to listen—she wanted to touch him, hug him, shelter him in the warmth of her body and her love. She did love him, would love him forever. She was a warm enveloping flame to keep what the other one had done to him from even grazing his skin.

"I'm coming over."

"No, wait . . . I don't know where they're taking her . . ."

"It doesn't matter. I'm coming over to your house. I want to be with you. I'm on my way."

She was pelted with questions from her father, her mother, her brother as she made her way to the front door.

"What's going on, Estelita?"

"Is someone sick?"

"Are you going over to Lucky's? I'll take you . . ."

"That crazy woman killed herself. Let me by."

"What crazy woman? The mother?"

"But . . . how? When? Do they need help?"

"What a vile woman. Doing such a thing to the boy!"

"Mom! Do you really think this is the time?"

"Sorry honey. But who called her a 'crazy woman'? Wasn't that you?"

"So unrefined," Sylvia had said when Lucky ran out of excuses not to introduce them to her. He'd had no trouble bringing Estela home when they'd first started dating. But it was a long way from there to introducing Sylvia to the whole family. On the one hand, she was mortified that Jaime had been immediately introduced and accepted into the Berrondo family and at the same time, she wondered what they were hiding from her. The girl was pretty, presentable, intelligent. Of course, she'd have selected someone else . . . This train of thought made her smile. As with any mother of a son none of them would really suit . . . but suddenly she was sobered by the thought that maybe it was the other way around. Maybe there was nothing monstrous or shameful about the Berrondos—maybe Lucky was trying to hide her? The notion became an obsession. She, the highly educated attorney Sylvia Meyer, wasn't she worthy of being introduced to the girlfriend's family?

In fact, what Lucky was afraid of was the lapidary assessment. He didn't argue. He would never make Sylvia understand that if he had to choose between culture and warmth, he'd choose warmth, once it had been turned in his direction.

He welcomed Estela with his whole body, as if to melt into the solidity of a generous woman, always open to him. She stroked his face, his eyes. Taking him by the waist she guided him to the bed, made him lie down, closed the blinds, and curled up beside him without speaking, transmitting the heat of the living through her warm lips. Estela had never felt any sympathy toward Sylvia, even though the latter had treated her cordially, almost affectionately. The things Lucas had told her carried more weight, even more so on those occasions when she had seen with her own eyes the damage Sylvia wreaked on her son. In Estela's opinion, the other woman was a malevolent being, tyrannical, abusive, and pitiless—a being, not a woman, a freak of nature. Lucky was who he was not thanks to his mother, but despite his mother.

How many times had he showed up at Estela's, his hands clenched into fists, barely containing his tears after some scene in which Sylvia had succeeded in beating him down, making him feel incapable, an airhead, not even sure of his own name! And she, Estela, would pick up the pieces, restore his status as a man, even as her hatred for the other grew and she wished her far away from their lives . . . without admitting it even to herself, she wished she were dead.

As if echoing her thoughts, Lucas' voice startled her.

"She's dead now."

"Yes, but she didn't do you much good when she was alive."

"It doesn't matter. I cannot tolerate what she did. I can't stomach it."

"Because it's a sin you mean."

"No, she didn't believe in all that. I mean what she did in life, how she hurt herself, every single minute, with no quarter. The suffering."

"And what she made you suffer."

"You don't get it. I didn't get it either. Making us suffer, my old man and me, just added to her own suffering. It didn't matter where she aimed the poison. In the end, it was always against herself."

"How do you know? Did she ever tell you?"

"No. She didn't talk to me. Or I didn't talk to her, for all I know. I didn't know her. I don't think anybody knew her."

Estela prudently held her silence. This stuff about not knowing your own mother was beyond the bounds of her comprehension. In her simple world, acts were love. She knew her parents well, loved them immensely, and felt protected by the love and care they had always given her. The relationships in Lucas' family were, to put it mildly, twisted. As she stroked his forehead, suggesting he sleep a little to gain strength before the wake, she wished with all her being that Sylvia dead would not be as or even more problematic than she had been in life.

The telephone wrenched them both from a restless sleep of intertwined arms and hair, devoid of images or thought.

"Lucky?"

"Yeah, Dad"

"Write this down. We have to let certain people know and ask them to call the others. I'll give you the list. If anyone else occurs to you, add them. The numbers are in your Mom's agenda."

"But I . . . wouldn't it be better if you called?"

"It isn't practical. I'm in a booth with only one working telephone and twenty poor slobs standing in line. And besides, it wouldn't be right. I haven't talked to those people for years. Write."

Moving soundlessly, Estela had risen and located pad and pen. So Jaime had turned practical all the sudden?

"Are you writing?"

"Yes, go ahead."

"Silvina, Inés, Sofía, Clara, Francisco."

"Yes, go on."

"I can't think of anyone else. Your mother had so few friends! They'll know who else to notify. Give them the address. The burial is tomorrow morning, leaving here at 10:00. When you finish, come over."

"Okay. How do I get there?"

"Take the Pan-American. Look for the Filcar. And explain it to the others so they don't get lost. They're not used to these neighborhoods, probably don't even know they exist. And you, don't speed. Stay calm."

"Yeah, ciao."

Why did his father insist on confronting him with precisely those obstacles that loomed before him like an unscalable cliff? The agenda, was it in the room from where they had taken "that?" He hated to talk on the phone with his mother's friends—they were either standoffish or sugar sweet. And what to say to them? What would Jaime have arranged as to the cause of death? Why did they always place him smack in the middle of their messes?

"She isn't there any more Lucky," Estela reminded him gently. "Anyway, if you'd rather not, I'll go. And I can make the calls if you're not up to it."

"Let's go together," he decided. Then they saw the agenda on the telephone table where it had remained since the call to Garnet.

Estela opened it randomly and said to herself, "So many names. You can't understand any of it." There were endless lists, words crossed out, and arrows from cover to cover. There were numbers without names, misplaced annotations, cigarette burns.

"Who are all these people? Are you sure you only have to call five? That's it?"

Lucas shrugged.

"They're clients, colleagues, people who had something to do with my Mom's work. Like my old man said, she barely had any friends."

"But why?" Estela was astounded. "Everyone has friends . . . even the bad guys in the movies."

Innocent Estela. Lucas gave her a kiss on the cheek and concentrated on the list. What was there to explain? That Sylvia, the bad guy in this movie—the past tense came easily to him now—had been a difficult person, not very sociable, hypercritical of herself and others. That many respected or feared her, but they did not love her. That she did not inspire affection and, if it was offered, tended to reject it. Yet he remembered when he was very young, his parents used to go out with friends and frequently a pretty sizable group would come over for dinner, or a glass of wine, or coffee. Where were they now? When, how had they lost touch? Most likely Sylvia had pushed them out of her life, in pursuit of the self-fulfilling prophesy of her solitary being.

With a look of exasperation, he copied the five numbers onto a sheet of paper and passed it to Estela.

"Here, take it. You call. If they're not there, leave a message. If they answer, tell them you're not sure exactly what happened. Tell them you don't really know anything. Say I asked you to call them and then meet me over there. I'm going to take a shower. I feel . . . as if I fell into a cesspool."

Two hours later, they entered the funeral home hand in hand. SYLVIA MEYER—ROOM B. A flight of stairs and there was ROOM A discharging its affliction into the hallway. Between "excuse mes" and "sorries," they made their way to the entrance to Room B. A small reception area and a cubicle of sorts, with the gleaming casket under yellow neon lights. A solid nail marked the place where the cross had been removed.

No one.

"Where the hell is the old man hiding?" said Lucas indignantly. "Are they going to leave me alone here too?"

In other circumstances, Estela would have protested coyly, along the lines of "and what am I?"

"He must've stepped out to arrange something," she said instead, squeezing his hand tightly. "Let's sit down. There, by the door."

Lucas allowed himself to be guided. There were moments when he felt as if none of this were happening: "she" was going to burst in at any moment, with her deliberate walk, her knife-edged tone, saying, "*See? Let that be a lesson to you!*" And then his eyes would stray toward the casket and "she" was that; she was no longer. And he needed her: to hate her, to have her with him, to love her, a little, sometimes. Doubled over with nausea, he needed to ask her how and why she had abandoned him.

Jaime entered the room silently, with a small bouquet of spring flowers. He placed them on the casket where he calculated her hands would be and then approached Lucas and Estela, his eyes red and swollen.

Lucas' internal discourse became a question, with no thought for continuity.

"So, did you still love her?"

"Always, even when she turned into a quivering mass of rejection and I no longer understood her—if I ever did understand her that is—I still loved her. I love her."

"Then why did you leave? Why didn't you help her?"

Jaime, half sigh half sob, retreated to the opposite wall. It wasn't the time. You can't explain a whole lifetime in front of a mute witness who contradicts you from the unassailable reality of death.

Lucas was getting impatient.

"So isn't anyone going to come? Doesn't anyone care?"

There was no response. Jaime did not dare to tell him that yes, a few people would come all in good time, either out of curiosity or to return the favor since Sylvia had been present for all of their losses. Or that a few would be trying to recover from the shock in order to put up a stronger front. All in good time.

Chapter V

THE FRIENDS

SILVINA

"Mom, can I invite Sylvia over to play? And can she stay for dinner? And spend the night? Tomorrow's Saturday . . ."

Silvina, a chubby whirlwind of blond braids, pranced around her mother on one foot, firing off questions: yes, yes, yes, if her mother says it's okay. You're making me dizzy, girl!

A dash for the phone at the other end of the immense house and then back again. A breathless "she says yes except her mom can't bring her because she's busy but if we can go pick her up she'll let her. Can we go Mom? Can we go get her?"

It was nearly always the same story. Sylvia's mother, with a degree in humanities, a lecturer and political activist, was rarely at home and when she was, she was busy. Occasionally she took Sylvia to one of her little friends' houses, depositing her at the door and vanishing instantly in the same taxi that had brought them, a whirl of wide skirts and French perfume. The other mothers criticized her, secretly envious. She was, if not famous, then well known. But the child went from school to French class, then on to painting class and from there to dance, hanging from the hand of the live-in nanny. After all the back and forthing, she was relegated to her toys and to await her mother, who would take ten minutes to change, only to announce they shouldn't wait on her for dinner. As she selected her outfit, she'd issue precise instructions: Sylvia should eat at eight. And none of that nonsense about leaving the light on for such a grown up eight-year-old.

"But Ma'am, the child is afraid. She's been crying a lot at night, ever since her father left . . ."

"Ridiculous. You just shut the door and let her cry it out. She'll fall asleep eventually. One has to be firm with children."

"Yes Ma'am," (poor little Sylvia, as long as she doesn't die drowned in her own tears from crying so much).

The live-in nanny—always a new one, hard to remember their names since none of them could put up with the mistress's changing moods for long—felt sorry for the child. The children in other homes where she'd worked were mischievous, smart mouths, tricky, tattletales (I'll tell my mom on you), but they were kids—it oozed from their pores—all curiosity, eagerness to play nonstop, to be every place at once, tantrums, prattling and fussiness.

But Sylvia, in contrast, was odd. Poor Sylvita.

Poor Sylvita, clutching her pillow, drenching it with tears and snot and saliva, fearing her mother would come and find her awake.

It happened sometimes. And then her mother would pull her out from under the covers, sit her down on her lap and interrogate her.

"Let's see now. Tell me why you're crying."

"I don't know."

"Yes you do. Tell me why. You're not going back to bed until you tell me."

And Sylvia would invent some story, a nightmare, anything to escape her mother's grasp. The truth was she could not put into words why she cried. She intuited that she cried about everything, unable to break it down. But her mother had not accepted the answer the one time she had whispered it.

"What is 'everything'? I want you to explain it to me," she'd insisted, as the tears flowed out, uncontainable, and Sylvia's body shook violently like a rag doll and she'd ended up hiccupping in vomit and saying she was sorry. "I'm sorry Mommy, I'm sorry."

At this point, the mother would call the nanny.

"Clean all this up for me. Change her bed and have her lie down. The girl is hysterical."

The nanny shared these scenes with Sylvia's friends' nannies clustered around the school entrance. They in turn passed it along to their employers, massaging every detail, and the chorus of "poor Sylvia" ascended to the heavens. But who was going to get in the middle of it?

Night after night, Sylvia lulled herself to sleep between sobs: lullaby my sunshine, lullaby my little heart. That was the only part she remembered from hearing Silvina's mother sing it to her new baby.

"What shall we play?"

"Uh, I don't know . . . Statues?"

"Oh come on. You always win. I don't know how you manage to stay so still for so long."

"And you, you never stay quiet ever. How do you do it?" Silvina cracked up laughing.

"My mom calls me a little top!"

But they played statues, Ludo, charades, and dress up, falling off the spiky heels of the pumps Silvina's mom lent them.

At night, across the twin beds, Silvina got up her nerve to ask.

"Sylvita, why did your Dad go away?"

"I don't know . . . probably because I didn't behave myself."

"What do you mean didn't behave yourself? The teacher always holds you up as the example!"

"Well, because I don't like to eat and when they take me to birthday parties or first communions I don't play with the other kids . . ."

"And your Dad gets mad?"

"No, my Mom gets mad."

"So why didn't your Mom leave?"

"I don't know . . ."

Silvina could not grasp this line of reasoning. *"It's the grown up stuff they say you'll understand when you're older,"* she thought. She wrapped herself up in the sheets. Before falling asleep, she asked.

"Sylvita, do you miss your Dad?"

"Yeah . . . I mean, he takes me out and all but it isn't the same. I want him to take me to live with him."

"And he doesn't want to?"

"He says I'm better off with my Mom."

Silvina was remembering this and a lot of other things as she decided whether she'd go to the funeral alone or with her husband. She could not digest the news. Sylvia and she had been very close, until Silvina had gotten married and left the university. Sylvia and Esteban, her husband, had taken a mutual dislike to each other that made it hard to stay in close touch.

"That girl is incredibly stuck up," Esteban crucified her the day they met.

"But how can you say that? You didn't exchange more than two words!"

"That's why. She thinks it's not worth her time to talk to me. 'What an imbecile,' she must be thinking."

Silvina made no effort to stand up for her friend. To be honest, Sylvia's boyfriends weren't anything like Esteban. So she preserved their friendship by taking advantage of the moments when Esteban didn't need her: half hours in fashionable cafés and long chats over the phone abruptly curtailed by a "Silvina, hang up. Whatever you have in the oven is burning."

And yet they'd stuck together through pregnancies, childbirth, reversals of fortune, Silvina's health problems, and Sylvia's melancholy, the melancholy apparent in her cynical comments about everything, although she took care not to hurt Silvina in terms of what she believed in and loved.

Sylvia, who could do anything, was dead?

Estela had given her no explanations. Actually, she'd been evasive, awkward even.

The how did not concern Esteban.

"That's life, Silvina. Remember my brother who was only thirty when he died? Come on, get dressed and I'll drive you. I feel bad for Jaime. It's going to be tough on him."

"What does Jaime have to do with it? They divorced ages ago."

"But before that, she messed him up. He's a good guy, Jaime. He deserved better than that steam roller."

Silvina was indignant.

"You're forgetting the shitty life he gave her. When they were going to auction off the house, and when . . ."

"Shh, stop yelling at me. It would have been different with another woman."

"The same old story, Esteban? We women are always to blame?"

"For everything good and everything bad. Yes. Let's go. Did you bring the address? I have no idea where this place is."

What he did not say was that Sylvia most certainly had chosen the place herself, just for the hell of it.

FRANCISCO

He removed fogged up eyeglasses, rubbing his dark, myopic eyes with the thumb and forefinger of his left hand in a typical gesture that Sylvia never failed to point out to him when they were working together on a case.

"You're already throwing in the towel," she'd say, half in jest, half in reproach.

It actually was his way of showing his exhaustion, but today she truly would have been right. How to live without her? And yet she'd never been his. He'd never mustered the courage to tell her he loved her because it seemed irrational to him. Just seeing her and hearing her voice in the first postgraduate class she'd taught had produced a physical reaction in him, something he didn't believe he could feel—he, all calculation and rationality. That night and for many nights thereafter he'd dreamed about her, about making love with a degree of pleasure he'd felt with none of his partners, steady or occasional.

At the end of the course, Francisco approached the desk where she was gathering her notes into a folder. He wanted to ask for some more detail about a thorny issue in one of the verdicts they'd analyzed. She'd rebuffed him gently.

"It's a rather involved subject," and, glancing at her watch she added, "I have to be somewhere in fifteen minutes."

With an audacity he hardly recognized in himself, he proposed they have dinner together one night, so they'd have more time. She refused without glancing up.

"But we can have coffee next week, after exams. Friday at seven. Does that work for you?"

"Perfect. I'll pick you up at . . . ?"

"No, no. Let's meet at the Petit Colón."

"Thank you, Ms. Meyer, until Friday then."

"At seven," she reminded him, leaving quickly, barely acknowledging a small group still chatting in the doorway of the lecture hall.

"She knows a lot."

"She's a robot."

". . . when she doesn't like what you're saying . . ."

". . . not very feminine . . ."

"How harshly they judged her!" he thought on the way to his car. But did he really know any different? Yes, of course he did. He could glimpse the depth behind the poker face, the passion for her work that shone through in each analysis, case by case. She was one of those rare professors who did not just parrot textbooks or critics. She offered her own ideas. The woman must be equally deep and generous and he wanted the chance to reveal the treasure he believed he could glimpse in some less measured gesture or tone of voice.

On the Friday in question he was seated in the café a half hour early, mentally rehearsing ways to interest her, to get her interested in him. Absorbed in the high points of a trip to India that surely would interest Ms. Meyer he suddenly noticed her standing by the table, smiling at him.

Francisco jumped up so quickly and awkwardly he upset his chair, bumping into a waiter bearing a full tray in his attempt to right it.

She raised her eyebrows, just as she did when she disapproved of an interpretation offered by one of her students during a class discussion.

"She gives you the look that makes you wish the earth would swallow you whole," they said.

He had not been subject to that particular look, until now. It was fire and ice, question and contempt. It discouraged any attempt at explanation.

"Ms. Meyer . . ."

She removed her coat without allowing him to assist her and sat down.

Sylvia said, "We've moved on to the next stage right? If you've finished playing with the chair"—ouch, the mocking look—"then order coffee and mineral water. Good, now let's see. About the verdict you were having trouble with . . ."

She spoke with precision, quoting, paraphrasing, with the self assurance of one who knows she knows it.

He followed her effortlessly, all the while wishing she'd wrap it up so he could spring his own trap-pretext and penetrate the universe of Sylvia the woman.

"Is it clear now?"

"Very clear. But I wonder . . ."

"Don't wonder so much, Francisco. It isn't good to go round and round about other people's work. Accept it, and if you can, use it as a point of departure to develop something new. In the end, you're going to discover that the cat only has four paws. The fifth is just the first one on a new cat, right?"

He studied her with vague apprehension, unable to decide whether Sylvia had a strange sense of humor or whether she was calling him an idiot. Meanwhile, she forged ahead with her own questions.

"Tell me. You're obviously not from Buenos Aires. Where are you from?"

So he told her about his childhood in Córdoba, how he'd come to feel suffocated by the rigid society surrounding him, about his decision to study law in Buenos Aires.

"It must have taken awhile to get used to it," Sylvia remarked. We're pretty hard on people from the provinces here."

"It was difficult at first. But I was top in my class and was admitted to Yale. By the time I returned at the beginning of the year, I was a citizen of the world, although I didn't lose my accent I guess," and he smiled, enjoying Sylvia's surprise.

"But what is a Yale graduate doing wasting his time in a second-rate postgraduate program?"

"Getting reacclimated, I suppose. And you're not second-rate. If you knew how much my point of view has been changed by things you've said . . . When you said the expulsion of what is different is one of society's self preservation mechanisms, it made me think . . ."

Sylvia was no longer paying attention. She panicked whenever anyone told her that her words had changed other people's lives. She never recalled saying the things they repeated back to her like some sort of magic, sounds altering reality. She supposed that these people weren't making it up and yet, how could she have forgotten? Perhaps to free herself from the responsibility associated with unintentionally influencing other people's destinies? It had happened over and over again: someone attributed to her the power to cement destinies, to facilitate access to the unapproachable as if she were an oracular image from some remote era dominated by wisdom and knowledge. How could they be so confused? Or maybe she was the one who was confused, confused by others who inserted her between the pages of the philosophers and echoes of the commonplace?

"Do you agree?" She heard Francisco's voice as if from another world, yanking her abruptly back to the here and now.

"Excuse me?"

"If you are in agreement with Kelsey."

"Oh, well, it's one way of looking at the issue."

I'm boring her, Francisco thought. I should tell her about India.

But he did not get the chance. Sylvia rose, saying:

"It's very late. Thank you for a very nice evening," as she gathered her things and extended her hand to him.

"Can we do it again?" he asked hopefully.

"Of course, when I return from my honeymoon. I am getting married next week. We can organize an outing with my husband. I am sure you'll enjoy each other's company."

She spoke offhandedly, as if discussing a routine matter of no particular import. She gave him her card and left.

Francisco had not fully assimilated the news. It was the end of the fantasy, coupled with the conviction that all along she'd been perfectly aware he was after something else, in the guise of professional interest.

He spent the next two weeks hating her and desiring her, changing his mind like a tie. I wouldn't even consider calling her. I'll definitely call today. Today dissolved into tomorrow and tomorrow into no.

Several months later, as he was leaving the theater with a friend he had the sensation his neck was burning. He turned abruptly and there was Sylvia standing behind him next to a tall nice-looking young man. And the knife-edged stare and the half-smile.

She did not greet him right away. Addressing her companion, she said,

"Jaime, remember the brilliant lawyer I told you about from my postgraduate class? Well here he is. Francisco Rossi, Jaime Galván, my husband."

Jaime studied him with a curiosity that struck him as insolent. What would she have said to her husband? They'd probably laughed together over the classic case of the love-struck student. After several minutes of chitchat about the play, Sylvia threw down the gauntlet.

"Come have dinner with us on Friday. We have a lot to talk about."

Jaime wrote down the address and the home telephone number and Francisco, confused as much by the familiarity of her tone as by the invitation, watched them disappear into the crowd.

And then came the inevitable question. His friend wanted to know who they were, so he provided a terse explanation that obviously didn't cut it.

"Strange," commented his friend.

"What's so strange about it?

"I don't know. She is, I guess."

On Friday—the sole guest at a delicious dinner prepared by Sylvia—Francisco had the opportunity to converse with Jaime during the long intervals when she left them alone to attend to something in the kitchen.

A good guy, Jaime. He never let on that Sylvia and he might have talked about him. If they had that is. But it didn't really matter now. An intelligent, informed guy, this Jaime, though not nearly as deep as she was. The heart has its reasons. How stupid. Trying to accept the situation with something as mundane as that old saw.

The proposal came with the coffee.

"Francisco, would you like to work with me?"

"Well, I don't know. I'm not sure I can." The odd thing was he'd guessed she was going to say just that. He'd rehearsed his answers a thousand times, affirmative, negative, uncertain. When the actual question came, the air left his chest and his feet were like lead, anchoring him to the chair.

"Think about it," she continued, without pressuring him. I am not proposing a partnership, but lots of cases come through my office and you would be independent and free to choose your own."

"She's never been interested in working with someone else," interjected Jaime. "She must have a tremendous amount of respect for you."

Francisco left, trying not to give the impression he was fleeing. He'd promised her an answer without specifying when, knowing already it was yes. He wanted to see her every day, to share with her a physical and intellectual space he wouldn't have to share with her husband.

His hopes had been rekindled when the couple had separated. She, however, had begun to pull away, withdraw, almost shrink into herself, and she had refused to discuss her personal life.

Now she had abandoned him. No, betrayed him.

Did she ever give you any reason to believe . . . ? inquired a small voice inside him. *No, never. She never saw anything else in me but a brain.*

CLARA

Mechanically rummaging through the closet in search of a comfortable pair of shoes, Clara talked to herself out loud, as was her custom when she was perplexed. *Why am I not surprised? I don't know what story they're going to come up with, but I'm sure she killed herself. For a while now you could see it in her face when she thought no one was looking. How many times did I try to talk to her and she'd just cut me off.*

I'm fine, she'd say. And if I insisted, she'd stop answering my calls, she wouldn't return my messages, wouldn't open the door even if I rang the doorbell until the house shuddered.

Shoes in hand, she sat down on a hammock chair, resting her head on the broad caned frame. Sylvia had been much younger than she. Actually, Clara met her mother first, at a party event during which they'd become embroiled in a heated dispute. Each taking the other's measure, they were like two enraged bulls, neither one willing to cede ground. With tremendous diplomacy, the moderator had guided the debate to a close. Seated on either side of him, they'd eyed each other with disdain, a powerful desire to annihilate the other colored by a certain fascination at meeting one's match.

They continued to run into each other and out of an utter lack of agreement on every subject grew a friendship based on admiration for an intelligence that penetrated the most abstract realms, a type of intelligence Clara had always assumed was inherent only to certain men and that Sylvia's mother, Laura, had thought belonged exclusively to her.

Clara knew who Laura was, yet she had an image in her mind that once her public activities were concluded, she hung herself up in the closet alongside her impeccable clothing, ready to begin anew the following day. At some point, however, Laura let slip a comment,

"Wait for me a second. I have to call home to see if my daughter has arrived."

Clara's astonishment was almost comic.

"You have a daughter?"

"You didn't know that? I'll be right back."

Laura made a brief call and hung up after a couple of monosyllables.

"Where were we?" she said, picking up some galley proofs for the next electoral campaign.

"We were saying that you have a daughter."

"Yes, well, most people have children don't they?"

"No, Laura. I don't. Tell me her name, what's she like, what does she do . . . ?"

In Laura's mind, Sylvia was not a topic of conversation, but she deigned to respond because she was certain Clara would harp on it until she found out what she wanted to know.

"Her name is Sylvia and she'll be fifteen at the end of the month. She's neither pretty nor ugly, she goes to high school, takes a couple of other classes . . . I'd say she's fairly intelligent, but scattered. And quiet, but rebellious. It isn't easy to deal with her, I'll tell you that. When her dad was around, he defended her no matter what she did. Since the separation, I'd swear he's been filling her head against me."

"Laura . . . do you love her? No offense, please."

Laura resented the intrusion. What would Clara know about what was involved in loving a child?

Falling back on her good manners she said, "If I didn't love her my life would be a lot simpler."

Clara probed no further.

"I'd like to meet her."

"Certainly, although I cannot imagine what you'd have in common."

They agreed to have tea at Laura's house that weekend.

A small apartment, tastefully furnished. Works by prominent painters adorned the walls, all dedicated to the owner. After admiring the apartment, the library in particular, Clara asked after Sylvia.

"I'll call her as soon as the tea is ready."

"Sylvita! Clara is here . . ."

From the side doorway emerged the figure of a tall, awkward teenager with unruly black hair that escaped from the barrettes attempting to restrain it. She wore thick-framed glasses and when she sat down at the table and revealed her hands, Clara noted that the nails were gnawed away and the cuticles damaged. The visitor tried to engage the girl, but Laura insisted on being the center of attention, answering for Sylvia, even discussing her as if she were not there.

"Did you know, Sylvia, that you're going to the same high school I attended?"

"No, we were not aware of that," interjected Laura as she passed around the cups. "I imagine in your day the school was in better shape, because nowadays, it seems as if they are closing early every other day 'because the roof is in disrepair.' It's shameful!"

"Oh it was always like that. Who is the principal, Sylvia?"

Laura again.

"Angelina Bertoldi."

"?"

"Politics. Sylvia please, get your hair out of your face! Between those horrible glasses and that hair, I've told her a hundred times she needs to get it cut, because it isn't of the type one can wear long, it hides her face. That must be why she doesn't eat: she can't find her mouth."

"Mom, please!"

"Well, isn't it the truth? You can't imagine what a chore it is trying to get this child to eat. But getting back to Bertoldi . . ."

Family tree, the life and times.

Clara felt a surge of sympathy for the stifled girl. How difficult to be the daughter of this mother! She decided to invite her over to her house, get to know her. It wouldn't be all hair, glasses, and silence.

When she finally did so, she ran smack into Laura's resistance.

"I can't fathom what a woman like you sees in the little brat."

But she allowed her to go on the condition that she return home before dark.

Clara earned the trust and devotion of Sylvia, who devoured

everything the older woman read and bombarded her with questions. When the age difference balanced out, the friendship would be cemented on an equal footing, while Laura was relegated, not without protest.

"I do not understand why you're so big on my daughter," she pointed out to Clara when they ran into each other in the course of their activities. Clara would smile and shrug her shoulders. *If you'd just pay a little attention to her, you'd get it*, she thought.

Clara helped bring about a lot of changes in Sylvia. *I was so happy when she married Jaime and when they had Lucky,* she said to herself, pulling shoes on and off her feet. *But there was always something very dark underneath it all, something Estrada either overlooked or didn't dare touch. And the others who treated her after that—terrible. It seemed as if they were pushing her to the other side. Poor Sylvia, the horrible things she must have gone through.*

INÉS

"Yes, Sylvia . . . Sylvia Meyer."

Inés paced about the house with the cordless phone on call . . . twenty? "No, I don't know how it happened. I called two or three places but there was no answer, or maybe they've already headed over there . . . And yes, I do think you should go . . . There's nothing more depressing than a wake with no people . . . It doesn't matter that you hardly knew her . . . of course, it's different for me—like a nephew, I'd say . . . I understand. No don't expect me to call to tell you about it. Talking about wakes gives me the chills. Yes. Talk to you later."

At thirteen, with perfect features and a woman's figure, Inés had been the undisputed leader of freshman cohort "A". It was a closed circle that had formed in the practicum department of the most prestigious teacher training school. Compact in structure and solidified into rigidly defined roles, there was no room for anyone else. Sylvia had arrived with a special pass from the ministry. After formation and the Aurora, she walked into the crowded classroom where most everyone already was seated three to a double bench. Moving to the back of the room, she asked,

"May I sit with you? There's no other seat . . ."

The occupants of the bench looked her up and down, then arched their eyebrows toward Inés on the adjacent bench. Inés assented with a slight nod. There would be time later to find out who the intruder was.

Wordlessly, the girls slid over to make room for her. Sylvia did not thank them, nor did she open her mouth during the entire class. Inés did not take her eyes off her for a minute. She wanted to make her nervous in preparation for an attack at recess.

When the bell rang, they headed out to the courtyard, chatting and laughing. Inés noticed that Sylvia had remained in her seat and quickly murmured something to the teacher, whose voice echoed in the empty classroom.

"No one remains in the classroom during recess. Outside, let's go."

Sylvia went out. She remained standing in a corner, conscious that she was being ignored. Inés stepped up to her smartly, flanked by her deputies Gabriela and Nani. Planting herself directly in front of her, arms crossed and legs apart, she stared straight down at her from her full height of 5 foot 7 inches:

"What is your name?"

"Sylvia, Sylvia Meyer."

"You don't look like a Sylvia," retorted Gabriela and Nani in unison.

"No, you don't look like a Sylvia."

"So what's your name?" Sylvia queried her.

The expressions of the three girls went from astounded, to horrified, to incredulous. Who didn't know that Inés was INÉS, the boss, the terror of the school, the nemesis even of the teachers who considered themselves *au courant*.

Nani responded hastily.

"Her name is Inés."

Sylvia gave her the once over with the icy stare that would become her trademark, and said softly, so the others had to lean in to hear her:

"And who do you think you are, Cortés, so you need a 'tongue'? You don't look like an Inés either. But this," she gestured toward Nani, "must be 'Marina'."

And turning on her heel, she walked away.

All the girls had heard this exchange since, as soon as they'd seen Inés approach the new girl, the courtyard had fallen into a silence that even the strictest teacher failed to achieve.

What would happen now? Most of them hadn't the faintest idea what Cortés had to do with it, but it was clear that Inés had been insulted. They prepared to isolate the new girl once and for all. From this day forward she would never stop regretting the moment in which it had occurred to her to butt into "their" school. They were even more mystified when Inés let loose a guffaw and, crossing the courtyard in a snap, took her by the shoulders and looked her square in the eyes.

"You're all right," she said. "I want us to be friends, okay?" And right then and there, the two girls embraced and Sylvia became one of them. It was never clear to them what had happened, in part because Inés never bothered to explain. As they forged a relationship of unconditional affection on Inés' side and astonishment on Sylvia's—what was so special about her that someone would like her so much?—, they shared their stories.

Inés' parents were also divorced. She didn't like her father, whose departure she considered a betrayal, and she had a love-hate relationship with her mother, who was a domineering know-it-all, much like Sylvia's.

Inés was a bundle of unbridled passions, first diving dangerously into politics and then, at age 17, into the arms of a much older, married man. Iván Terzoff, a famous writer, had insisted that it was imperative to keep the relationship a secret to conserve the possibility of a future together.

Inés regarded Sylvia as her other half, her alter ego—there were no secrets with her. Sylvia was frightened by the excesses of physical passion that Inés described to her in infinite detail.

Shaking her head, she'd ask out loud, "But how can you just give yourself over like that?"

And Inés would smile sympathetically saying, "That's love, Sylvia. Giving of yourself. Blind trust. The knowledge they would never hurt you."

Sylvia, caught between credulousness and skepticism, could only repeat, "Just be careful. It scares me."

"That's because you've never fallen in love. If you love me, you have to be happy for me."

Some time later, Inés dropped by her house to pick up some books and then rush off to her piano lesson only to find her mother blocking the stairway, her face stiff and contorted into barely contained fury.

"Mom! What is it? Dad again I guess . . ."

"Your father has more than accomplished his goal of shaming

me in front of everyone we know, running off with that snot-nosed little bitch. But you had to bring it full circle, playing the snot-nosed little bitch with a man old enough to be your father."

Inés didn't dare interrupt. Who . . . ? It couldn't have been Sylvia, in an ill-conceived attempt to protect her born of her own fear?

"This afternoon Iván Terzoff's wife paid me a visit. Do you know what she told me straight out? 'Make sure that daughter of yours leaves my husband in peace. And she shouldn't have any illusions that he'll separate from me. The reason is simple: he's used to the good life and the money, all the money, is mine. And he's comfortable, much too comfortable to give it all up and fend for himself. Either it is terminated discreetly, among family shall we say, or I can cause a major scandal to the effect of "like father like daughter." So talk to her. Goodbye.' I've never been so humiliated!" The slap flew through the air, leaving marks on Inés' cheek.

"This is over now, do you hear me? If I hear so much as a whisper about it you're in the street, where it would appear you were raised in the first place."

So many years later, waiting for the taxi that would take her to the wake, Inés smiled faintly. Things had changed so much! But then, she had been ahead of her time and Iván had been a coward—and comfortable just as his wife had proclaimed. Sylvia had been right to be afraid.

She'd lived abroad for a time, with the help of her mother who preferred not to see her. She had returned married to an Italian. They had two children whom she'd allowed him to take back to Italy after the divorce. She saw them once or twice a year.

There had been, and still were, plenty of men, but she was easily bored and they didn't insist.

Solitude with no man around gave Inés a sense of power. But solitude with no Sylvia . . . that she could not even imagine.

SOFÍA

When she hung up the phone, her knees were trembling and her teeth chattered uncontrollably. She shut herself inside the bathroom. Juan would be coming home from the office any minute and she didn't want him to see her in this state. Still utterly gorgeous even after fifty, she never let her husband see her unless she was perfectly attired and made up. She took several deep breaths until the trembling ceased. She washed her face and reapplied foundation, eyeliner, and mascara. "I will not cry, she repeated, clenching her muscles. *My soul is in pieces but I will not cry. Why didn't I say something? Because they never say anything either. I could talk to Jaime about it . . . but I'm not even sure he cares. I never could talk to Lucas. I'll never forget the time he said all of his mother's friends were crazy. And I'm probably not even thinking straight. No. Not now.*

They'd met on a train from Paris to Versailles, so crowded there was no chance to feel nostalgic about the western port line back home.

Sylvia, whose French was passable, couldn't get even close to the door in any language. Sofía, who was also getting off there, needed only her sparkling smile and shining green eyes to open before her a magic corridor amid exclamations of approval. She quickly grabbed Sylvia by the arm and they were soon looking at each other and laughing on the platform of the tiny station.

Sylvia was sure Sofía was French.

"Je vous remerci," she began, but was cut short by Sofía's guffaws.

"I don't understand a word of French," she yelled over the roar of the locomotive, "and you're more Argentine than *mate*, no?"

They sat down on a bench to wait for the lone taxi, which was obliged to make several trips, as the French passengers did not share cabs. Sylvia told her she was studying in Rome on a scholarship and taking a week's vacation in Paris. Sofía was traveling around Europe. It had been a gift from her parents, a year of sabbatical before embarking on her career.

Following the trip to Versailles, they became inseparable. Sophia alighted in Paris once a month, dragging Sylvia out on adventures she would never have dared undertake alone: strip clubs, or truck stop cafés where you sat on narrow benches before long tables, sharing the bread, cheese, and wine, and where there was always plenty of advice for the Argentine girls, who'd been adopted from the first day.

From other countries, Sofía would require her presence for the weekend.

"I'll meet you at the Vienna train station at 10:00 a.m. We have a date with two incredibly good-looking guys."

Sylvia would be reluctant, yet she forced herself to go and she usually had a good time.

Sofía was constantly falling in love. Sylvia merely kept a safe distance from the hands of her partner of the moment, without incurring in any direct offense. Why were all the guys so primitive? They didn't even bother to pretend, even for a moment, that they were interested in her and she was not about to resign herself to being nothing more than an escape valve.

"I can't believe you don't like any of them! Come on, just name one person who could get you out of your panties."

"Clint Eastwood."

"But that's like saying the man in the moon! It's completely impossible!" said an indignant Sofía.

"That's the whole point. I wouldn't know what to do with the possible."

Back in Buenos Aires, Sofía joined her father's architectural firm and started dating a colleague who directed the jobs. She inundated Sylvia with all of the marvels and fascination of "true love, the love of your life, the one that's forever." Sylvia listened to it all as one following the episodes of a soap opera, saying to herself even then, *"If she believes it, it exists. But not for me. Never for me."*

Waiting for Juan to go to the wake, Sofía remembered the occasions on which she had presented her with candidates, all of whom had been discarded with a curt gesture, similar to removing a piece of lint. Over the years, Sylvia had organized her own parade of disastrous lovers as Juan had put it, exploding one day out of pure emotion.

"Tell me Sylvia, are you aware of the fact that this guy is never going to marry you? Just like all the ones before him?"

"Perfectly well aware," was the completely unruffled response.

"So why don't you move on and find someone who's really available?"

"That's why," and seeing the desperation on both of their faces, she said soothingly, "I'm fine like I am. I really don't want you to worry about me."

Sofía didn't really believe her but neither could she spend her life trying to convince her there were better options.

When she'd announced she was going to marry Jaime, Sofía had thrown her a wedding shower. In her mind, the best things about Jaime had to do with what he wasn't: a crazy genius, a tortured intellectual, a divorce addict with kids all over the place, an arrogant brat. The whole rogues gallery.

56

When they separated—*"I can't do it any more,"* Sylvia had said by way of a preliminary explanation—Sofía and Juan had clung to the illusion that sooner or later they would reconcile. When the passage of time showed otherwise, Sofía had continued to insist, *"Sylvia moves slowly, but you'll see . . ."*

She'd never imagined she'd witness this ending. She couldn't stop the thoughts that drummed against her temples like a remorselessly wielded hammer. If she had been ill, why hadn't she said so? Or maybe she hadn't realized she was sick? Or? No, not that. Not Sylvia. But then, why that afternoon . . . ? No. Subconsciously, she borrowed Sylvia's own motto, *If you don't believe it, then it doesn't exist.*

Chapter VI

EUROPE

If Sofía only knew! Had it not been for her, Sylvia would have returned home without completing her scholarship. From Buenos Aires, Rome had seemed to her a well deserved reward for her dedication to her studies. She'd confronted her parents—in agreement for once in their overwhelming disapproval of the dangers that lay in wait for a girl out on her own in the world—telling them that she didn't need their approval. After years of their not giving her what she really wanted (but she'd wanted something that was something and wasn't anything) they weren't going to deprive her of the one thing she'd dreamed about since she'd first opened those books teeming with marvelous words through which her mind had recreated the history of Rome, the center of the universe. Why should they be so worried about what might befall a girl out on her own, when she'd always been on her own, and what they seemed to be so afraid of had already happened to her, though they didn't know it, because she'd never told them. What were they going to say to her? That it was her fault: "there must have been a reason" the time she'd gotten on the first floor elevator and just before pressing the button for her floor an unsightly individual with the appearance of a beggar had opened the door and squeezed inside, asking her in a completely normal voice . . . and then had stopped the elevator who knows where, had fallen to his knees and in an instant that had seemed to her an eternity, had lifted her skirts, pressing and grinding his greasy head against her sex, through her panties, as he (she'd understood this part only much later) masturbated with the hand that wasn't holding her in an iron grip. Just that, nothing more. She hadn't screamed, or cried, or pleaded. Suddenly she was alone again in the elevator, mute, with her twelve-year-old's pleated skirt a mess and a budding fear of Laura's reproaches: "so this is why I kill myself working, so you can be utterly careless with the clothes I buy for you." Of course, technically speaking, as a lawyer, Sylvia could catalog the incident with absolute authority. But however one chose to label it, she'd felt violated, and she had decided—so intuitive, so in charge of her solitary being for such a long time now and forever more—not to submit to a second violation by telling a mother who would eye her with distrust, with irritation, this daughter who always found a way to complicate her life, or a father who wouldn't know what to tell her, confounded as he was by the perversity of others. So they'd had to resign themselves to the fact that she was going to travel once they realized that she no longer stayed where they put her. Their fear of "the worst" that could befall her was quickly replaced with outward displays of pride directed toward anyone who might be interested in listening: their daughter, intelligent as she was, had won a scholarship and, in front of others, was leaving with their approval to add yet another badge to the family honor.

Rome truly was the center of the universe. But the Romans of the history books did not live there. The elites, Sylvia's classmates, were decadent, haughty, contemptuous, and ignorant. In the city of Julius Caesar, the princes numbered in the hundreds, and the counts in the thousands. Propped up solidly by their illustrious surnames, they did not deem it necessary to give society anything more than their calling card stamped with the respective crest. In one of the worst economic crises ever in the country, they strolled past the unemployed with an indifference bordering on blindness. The fact was, the poor did not exist; they were merely a blemish on the marvelous architecture of the palaces they, the NOBLES, had carefully hollowed out in order to provide themselves with all the modern comforts, conserving the exterior structures their forebears had erected so that their coats of arms would be exhibited in the imposing stone shields.

She bit her tongue to keep herself from screaming at them that you can't build a life on the merits of others, or that—and this was more difficult still—those surnames they were so proud of dated back to a caste of mercenaries who sold themselves to the highest bidder and were compensated with titles and land . But if they didn't know their own history, what was a foreigner come from the ends of the earth going to teach them? And doubly a foreigner at that, because to top it all off she was Jewish? No, they were tolerant, but only to a point. They were so tolerant that they had suggested she visit the great synagogue, such a gorgeous building, and well, too bad about the Germans, but the building, at least, had been saved.

The foreigners swarmed the streets, taking refuge behind their cameras and tracing the tourist circuits in an infantile merry-go-round. There were other Argentines as well. Sylvia avoided them as much as possible: invoking the hospitality of the motherland, which had taken in so many immigrants, they thought they were entitled to the world and they definitely stood out, indeed they did.

On May 25, all of the residents had been invited to a reception by the Ambassador to commemorate the anniversary of the revolution.

Reluctantly, Sylvia resigned herself to dressing up like a young lady and ascended the eternal marble staircase to a salon where famous artists mingled, although not as much with the foreign diplomats or anonymous people like her. Surrounded by a reverent group, the Cardinal Primate was striking in his mundane bearing under the silk biretta. After the national anthem had been sung, exquisite porcelain plates were distributed along with silver spoons to eat the traditional cake. Afterwards, some of the guests began to leave. Observing them go by, Sylvia recognized some of the signature names of the culture. Suddenly, the Cardinal appeared at the foot of the stairs with an agility inconceivable for a man of his age. For some reason, he was trying to delay them, waving his arms, his face florid, and his mouth issuing unintelligible murmurs from above.

Piqued with curiosity, Sylvia descended the stairs to join the group, and there she could hear the Cardinal's words quite clearly, although what she heard made no sense.

"The spoons, for the love of God, give back the spoons."

Only when the celebrities deigned to reach into the pockets of their tuxedos or their beaded purses, did she comprehend the reason for the minor upheaval.

One by one, the Cardinal collected the silver spoons smeared with sweet milk caramel that the ladies and gentlemen were taking with them as a "souvenir."

They certainly did stand out, those Argentines.

"If you only knew, Sofía, that if it hadn't been for you . . . !"

But Sylvia held her secrets very close to her heart and no Cardinal was going to make her take them out, smeared with sweet bitterness.

Chapter VII

CLOSED CASKET

After a lengthy deliberation, Estela's family decided they should go, to support Lucky and their own daughter.

In other circumstances there would not have been a second's hesitation. Their lives revolved around a calendar of births, baptisms, birthdays, visits to sick relatives and friends, funerals, and weddings. Those movements *en masse*—everyone went to all the ceremonies— came as naturally to them as breathing yet, with respect to Sylvia, they were not sure. The phrase Estela had used, "That crazy woman killed herself," echoed in their ears and they weren't exactly sure how to behave: should they let on that they knew the truth, inquire as if they knew nothing? It was beyond their comprehension that someone could actually commit suicide. In this case in particular they were indignant more than anything else, *"over what she did to Lucky. Is that being a good mother?"*

Once there, they found Estela arguing with Lucas in a low voice.

"What do you mean you're not going to tell your friends? Our friends?"

"No, they'll find out about it through the announcement."

"But it will be too late. The announcement comes out tomorrow. Don't you want to see them?"

Lucas was just one monolithic "no." Shame, anger, consternation, and above all, the glimmer of relief he didn't want to show through.

Estela retreated for a moment and murmured to her family, bunched up in a corner: "It was a heart attack. Got it?"

"But how, honey, when you said . . . ," began the mother, while the father raised his eyes to the ceiling as if to say, *"let's see if they can work this one out."*

"Yes, Mom, but this is the official version. What the family has decided on. Okay?"

"Don't you worry, honey. Those poor people have suffered enough. We're not going to make it worse. You just relax."

The Berrondos observed a few people trickle in. Some greeted each other, while others obviously were not acquainted. They hugged Jaime and Lucky. Jaime, emotional and shaky, hugged them back. Lucky seemed carved in stone.

It seemed to them that there were two groups: one very small, mostly women, who must be Sylvia's friends, and another, larger, group of men, whose nicely cut suits, sober ties, haircuts and designer sunglasses revealed them as the successful lawyers they surely were.

Some paused for a few moments next to the casket in silent prayer. One person brushed the wooden surface with a kiss. The women cried with dignity behind dark sunglasses. Two or three murmured with difficulty, as if they couldn't put the words together.

The Berrondos were able to glean fragments like *"It couldn't have been . . . ," " . . . perfectly healthy heart," ". . . that she killed herself."* They weren't going to be able to hide it, no matter how they tried to cover it up. Lucas was going to carry the stigma of a suicidal mother with him for the rest of his life, leaving in his wake a trail of assumptions, half truths, half lies, sharing with his father a *"there must have been a reason"* that would impale them with imagined and imaginary guilt.

There was a minor upheaval when an employee of the funeral home came in with a wreath proclaiming in large letters "Bar Association of the Federal Capital." Jaime hurried forward.

"No flowers."

"But Sir there's a little bouquet on the casket . . ."

"Yes, but those will be the only ones. Please leave these and any others that arrive outside."

And arrive they did. The professional associations and institutions followed through with the formalities. Nothing personal. A member had passed away. The rules were observed as usual.

At some point, Clara approached father and son to ask whether they were thinking of spending the night.

They looked at each other in confusion. It hadn't occurred to them.

"We're not sure yet," answered Jaime.

"Because if you'd like to go and get some rest, I have no problem staying," she assured them, "and Inés will probably keep me company."

"We'll let you know," Jaime repeated. "Come on, Lucas. Let's get some coffee."

They shut themselves inside the tiny kitchen to say out loud what should not be said. Sylvia alive had systematically refused affection, company. Of what use would it be to accompany Sylvia dead?

"Not me, no way," stipulated Lucas.

"I'd be invading her death, when she wouldn't even let me get near her when we were still together. It would be different with Clara . . ."

"You know what, Dad? Let Clara do whatever she wants. I'm leaving in a few minutes . . ."

"Home?"

"No, to Estela's. I'll go by the house to get some clean clothes and I'll be back tomorrow to go to the cemetery. I suggest you leave as well."

Jaime agreed. The friends and colleagues who had arrived so spaced out vanished suddenly, all at once.

Clara sent Jaime a questioning look, approaching with Inés and Francisco.

"If it's all right with you we'd like to stay."

"It really isn't necessary, but . . ."

"It would make me feel better," declared Francisco in a very low voice.

"That's fine then. I'll see you tomorrow."

Jaime said his goodbyes, glancing around for Lucas, but he was no longer there, nor were the Berrondos.

Downstairs he recalled that according to Sylvia's letter, he and Lucas were strangers. So maybe the ones who were going to keep her company were the closest ones?

Alone in the anteroom, the three guardians remained absorbed in their own thoughts for a long while.

They'd heard about each other, they'd come across each other on occasion, but there were no direct ties between them. Nonetheless, they felt strangely connected by their common loss. They didn't have to be careful about what they said, and when Clara spoke, either one of the others could have claimed her words as their own.

"Do you believe the heart attack story?"

"Frankly, it's not very clear. It wasn't the moment to ask a lot of questions, but didn't you get the impression that Jaime and Lucas were going on and on a bit too much?"

"I'm certain she killed herself." Francisco was so definite it made both women's skin crawl.

"Did she say something to you? You saw her most every day . . ."

"It was what she didn't say. She came and went like a shadow, she didn't speak, didn't eat . . . it was excruciating. You couldn't go near her. She left an aura of anguish floating in the air that was unbearable. And then she'd suddenly be attending to a client and her

63

expression would change, her voice, her posture, only to crumble again when the person left."

"But Silvina and Sofía were saying that they spoke often on the phone and she sounded good, upbeat. Speaking for myself, I often had the impression she was barely containing her tears, but she didn't let me in either. You know, I started having nightmares about her, dead of a thousand different causes. I never got up the nerve to tell her about them. I was afraid, how should I put it . . . afraid of giving her ideas," Inés almost didn't get out the sentence.

"Silvina and Sofía," snorted Clara, "never saw what was going on." They lived in their Barbie doll world and Sylvia was their eccentric friend. I'm not saying they didn't love her, but they took the dark, terrible side she had as a pose. I saw it in her from the time she was just a little thing. That's why I sent her to Estrada."

"The psychiatrist?" Inés was surprised.

"Yes, him, and others too."

"She never mentioned it." Now Francisco realized what was in those little bottles with the labels carefully removed in the office bathroom.

"But why?" Inés voice rose in pitch, bouncing off the smoked glass windows.

"Why did she go to the psychiatrist? I told you . . ." began Clara, but Francisco interrupted her gently.

"No, Clara. Why did she kill herself?"

"That we'll never know, unless Jaime and Lucas say something, assuming they have any idea, that is."

"I doubt it. Usually the closest ones, I'm talking about Lucky not Jaime, can't see what's right in front of their noses."

"You really care a lot about Lucky, don't you Clara?" confirmed Francisco.

"A lot. And so does Inés, I would say. You don't?"

"Lucas," Francisco made clear, "is a spoiled brat who shit colossally on his mother. And before you ask me, I'll tell you: I know because of what she didn't say."

"Poor Sylvia . . ." sighed Inés.

"Poor all three of them," corrected Clara. But she did not explain. It didn't matter any more.

Chapter VIII

THE CEMETERY

At nine o'clock the following morning a single car followed the hearse. For various reasons, Clara, Inés and Francisco were unwilling to go to the cemetery. Ultimately, cremation was too final an end. If they were not present perhaps they could conserve some part of Sylvia, the part each had known and loved, along with the pain of knowing it had been of no use to her—to her, untouched by love. That part they had not known.

The apartment on Calle Defensa was vacant for days, weeks, gathering dust, new cobwebs, rust stains around the leaky pipes.

Jaime tried to stay close to Lucas at first but, not getting much of a response, gradually became reabsorbed in his own life.

Lucas, an eternal guest at Estela's, did not mention Sylvia and postponed the opening of the estate papers until "later on." What was the rush? He was the sole heir to some possessions that were of no value whatsoever to him. On occasion his mother had bewailed the fact that Argentine law did not allow wills: the principle of the heir apparent governed. *"It's all well and good to leave bequests to those who love you—to those you love,"* she would say. And the letter, burnt to ashes, began to piece itself back together in the mind of the son. Sylvia had not mentioned the things that could not be destroyed, resigned to the fact that in the end, ownership would be passed on to him. But she had underscored her disapproval by asking them to get rid of her things and books, insisting she didn't want anyone else to have them. But who did she think she was anyway? Did she think people would be standing in line to get something that had belonged to her, as if she'd been a saint or miracle worker or something? Well then. Lucas felt as if the miracle resided in his not having succumbed all that time living with such a pernicious mother. At any rate, the candidate for canonization should be he.

One Sunday he jumped out of bed at an abnormally early hour for him. He began to dress and was just leaving when Estela intercepted him.

"Where are you going so early?"

"To clean."

"Your house. Wait, let me throw something on and I'll go with you."

"No, it's not that type of cleaning. I have to go alone. Don't wait for me. When I'm done, I'll call you."

Arriving at the place where he'd lived his entire life, it struck him as so depressing he thought he could feel a physical, diffuse pain running through him, threatening to take up residence in each part of his body, especially his hands—the hands he now needed for what he had come to do.

Then, strangely, out of the same pain he'd rejected, he could engage in a dialogue with Sylvia, with the marks of Sylvia, from inside him and without.

"We said you died of a heart attack. And you know, Mom? Now I'm not so sure it was a total lie that your heart killed you: a heart that died who knows when and started to poison your soul. A heart that exploded with fury and terror as it rotted away. We mistook it for something else. Is that what happened, Mom? Had your heart been so mistreated that you stopped it once and for all because you couldn't take it anymore?"

Lucas began to systematically dismantle Sylvia's room. He yanked off the sheets, blanket and bedspread and piled them in a corner of the hall. On top he heaped all the sheets stacked carelessly on the top shelf of an enormous closet. Then he emptied the clothes hangers and drawers where pullovers and t-shirts had been tossed together with underwear, ripped articles that somewhere along the line his mother was planning to take to the seamstress. He noted for the first time that many of the clothes had old stains on them, which appeared to be food and emitted a rank odor. These were the things Sylvia wore on a daily basis, yet he had not noticed their state of neglect before. Had others noticed? No, surely not. No one really looked at her. He imagined that for others, as for him, she had been the ironic mouth, a pair of eyes crowned with Medusa hair, disembodied, invisible although audible. He took out box after box of shoes, without bothering to open them. He took a plastic bag and emptied hoops, bracelets, chains, rings, and broaches into it. When would they be from? He did not recall having seen her wear anything but a cheap, simple watch, which was nowhere to be found. In another bag he dumped the contents of the bedside tables, without pausing to poke around in them. He gathered up all her purses, tying them together by the handles with a plastic cord. Like someone checking out of a hotel and wishing to make sure nothing had been left behind, he reopened all the doors and drawers. All that remained, in his imagination, was an air of filth, of age, of death.

As he washed his hands, he considered how to dispose of the pile of misery.

"Take it to the church I guess," he thought, allowing himself the pleasure of not putting the seat back down. Sylvia had hated it when he and Jaime left the seat up. She said it was the height of vulgarity. Lucas smiled mirthlessly. Such reproaches would not be bothering him any longer.

He looked for some more bags to empty the desk. Sitting before it, he swept aside the jumble of papers concealed behind the green leather top. On the right were three deep drawers. The first two contained files of utility bills. He left them where they were—they belonged to the house not to his mother. In the third drawer, he found an old wooden sewing box. He thought he remembered his paternal grandmother giving it to Sylvia for her birthday and she, in typical fashion, had considered it a piece of rubbish and had shoved it in there.

He hesitated to throw it out, because it was a souvenir from his grandmother. Jaime might even want it.

He had trouble opening it. Somehow the velvet edges had stuck together and he tried hard not to rip them. Finally, the sewing box opened to reveal, not spools and needles, but once again, papers. He was about to toss them without a glance, but taking them out, he could see they were dated and addressed to different people.

Once again Sylvia and her fucked up writings! Wasn't she going to leave him alone, even dead?

For an instant he thought about burning them, and then it occurred to him that perhaps the addressees had a right to know about these posthumous messages. But he wouldn't deliver them without reading them first. Surely they would be as hurtful as those horrible blue pages—but now Sylvia's ability to continue wounding with her most effective weapon depended on his whim.

He carried the box to his bed and began to read.

FIRST LETTER

October, 1985
Mother's Day

Mom:

I don't really have any other means of addressing you—I can't imagine calling you since you never responded and now, your memory gone but not your harshness, I don't really want to call you.

It's so easy for you to say 'I don't recall . . . ,' so easy for you to weave memories of things that never happened, in which you are featured as the loving mother, understanding and self-sacrificing, all so that this daughter, the only one of the three who survived ('I don't recall, were there others?') would have a happy life.

You built your life—and mine—upon lie after lie; lies that gradually dissipated, almost by chance, as I was able to put together fragments of conversations overheard at far too young an age to grasp their meaning; fragments that would be reinterpreted much later when, well-trained in your own harshness, I was no longer capable of forgiving you.

You said you were an only child but as an adult, you abandoned your younger brother to his fate, out of jealousy, because you believed grandmother loved him more than you. You banned him from the house, sick and with a child. Dad said he ended up in Paris, as so many other painters did; no one knows what became of him.

You kept his paintings, beautiful works, as long as grandmother was alive. It irritated you when people asked who had painted them; grandmother would cry and Dad would change the subject. After grandmother died, the paintings disappeared ('what paintings? . . . I don't recall . . .'). Your older sister, too weak to withstand your constant attacks, retreated to a convent. How ironic! The lineage of Judah finding refuge in the peace of Christ. No wonder you were horrified when I decided to baptize my son. I imagine you thought he would follow in my aunt's footsteps. I know she died. I also know that your family visited her, loved her, and made her happy behind your back. But I, her only niece, was deprived of an aunt who might possibly have loved me ('I had a sister? No . . . You must be confused.') The truth is, I am confused. When, in a moment of rebellion against your efforts to convince me that solitude was my fate, Dad mentioned my unfortunate siblings, one who lived only a few days, and the one you lost at nearly full term, falling on the theater stairs while attending an opening you could not miss without risking the criticism of your friends, you were beside yourself with fury and threatened to sue him for turning me against you through malicious libel ('I don't recall . . .'). All of these were things I did not witness firsthand. But now comes what is mine, what I can forgive you for least of all, what I can never forgive you for, ever, inasmuch as I am a creature of your making. I was eight years old. You took me on vacation to Mar del Plata because your friends would be there and you would have people to be with. One morning, as you were getting ready to go to the beach, telling me to hurry up because you'd miss the best hours of sun, I told you I didn't feel well. It was a repeat of the nighttime scenario, the pitiless questioning, my tears. Your final response, 'You're not going to ruin my vacation. If you're so sick, but nothing hurts, then you can just stay in bed until I get back.'

You picked up your raffia bag, your hat, your sunglasses, and you left, locking the door behind you.

My sobs intensified until I vomited; I wanted to die. At the time I didn't have a clear understanding of what it meant to stop living, but I knew it involved invisibility, that no one talked to you and you didn't have to answer. You disappeared. In the midst of it all, a maid heard me from the hallway, opened the door with her key, and became visibly upset.

'Where's your mom?' was the first thing she asked.

I managed to tell her you had gone to the beach. She made a strange gesture and touched my forehead. She immediately grabbed the telephone and called the manager.

'I'm in 510 and there's a little girl here burning up with fever. I found her alone . . . locked in. She says her mother's at the beach . . . let's see . . . wait a minute . . . Child, which beach did your Mom go to?'

I managed to blurt out Playa Grande.

'She says to Playa Grande . . . okay, that's fine.'

She hung up, sat down next to me on the bed, and holding me close said,

'They're going to send someone to find your Mom. It will take a little while, because Playa Grande is a big beach, but by calling out your Mom's name and that of the hotel, they'll find her. Meanwhile, I'm going to stay here with you and the doctor is going to come, okay?'

I think that I did not answer. The warm embrace of a perfect stranger was more important to me than the doctor, who came, ex-

amined me, and said nothing except that he wished to speak to my mother when she showed up.

When they finally found you and brought you back, Mom, you were furious. You practically shoved the maid out the door, telling her off for having dared to enter without permission.

As soon as we were alone—what I was most afraid of was being alone with you—you scolded me, counting on your carefully manicured fingers: first, I had made you look bad in front of your friends, who must have thought you were a bad mother who'd abandoned a sick child. Second, my only illness was my naughtiness, as usual. Third, you had had to put up with a sermon from the doctor on call, who'd diagnosed the incident as 'a severe anxiety attack' and had tried to interrogate you about the frequency of such episodes. Naturally you had informed him that he should mind his own business. 'But'—you warned me—'on top of the fact that your father takes no responsibility, you're going to behave yourself properly or I'll have you confined to boarding school. I'm leaving now, and make sure I don't find out you've caused another uproar.' After which you gathered up your things and left. This time you did not lock the door behind you.

('What an imagination for the love of God . . . I could never have done such a thing. In any event, I really don't recall.')

Determined that there would be no repeat of the experience, during the ensuing summers, if Dad could not take me on vacation you packed me off to the country home of some relative, expressly forbidding them from teaching me to ride a bicycle, swim, or skate 'because if anything were to happen to her, I'd die. She's all I've got.' You should have explained that I was the only thing you had to torture in this world.

And there the package stayed, alone, reading, while the other kids in the house and their friends did what kids did and laughed more or less openly about the stilted visitor who'd been so unceremoniously palmed off on them.

The question I heard most during that time, repeated in every possible tone of voice was, 'so when are you leaving?' And I wanted to go—but to the closest river, except I was terrified by the brown, muddy water and what might lurk beneath it, like snakes, for example. So I waited for you patiently, thankful for the distracted crumbs of affection from the adults and taking your hand resignedly when, tanned by the Pacific, or perhaps the Mediterranean sun, you came back for me, white, almost transparent. 'Don't let her out in the sun—she has terrible skin just like her father.'

When I reached adolescence, you erected a wall of terror around sex, all the while throwing in my face that you had not remarried 'because all men, sooner or later, think alike and it is my duty as a mother not to risk such a thing under my own roof.'

'If it weren't for you,' you'd say, 'I'd have a companion. . . I'd have made it in politics. . . I'd have saved money. But of course, when one has to educate a daughter, there are other priorities' ('I don't recall that . . .').

And the icing on the cake: when Lucas was about to be born and I was still laboring at home, before it was time to go to the hospital, the pain from the contractions caused me to scream. While Jaime talked to me, took my hands, put on music to distract me, you, slamming the door resoundingly, announced in a loud voice, 'I don't know why I have to put up with this. Why don't you just take her once and for all?'

There are more beads to string on this necklace, but you know me, I'm selfish.

This is my humble gift to you, on Mother's Day.

Sylvia

"And she didn't dare give it to her? Or she felt sorry for her?" exclaimed Lucas.

("Lucky, shall I tell you about . . ." Could this be what she'd wanted to tell him?)

On an impulse he went to look for a photograph album that had been stuck up at the top of a closet together with some other papers belonging to Grandmother Laura. Once they'd looked at it together, but he hadn't been interested in those old black and white photographs that illustrated the many successes of his grandmother. Now, gazing at it attentively, he noted that there were very few photos of Sylvia, three or four with Laura, a couple with the grandfather, and a couple of others just of her.

If Sylvia hadn't smiled much as far back as he could remember, it would seem she hadn't as a child either: from the park, to the zoo, to the beach, her thin face and large eyes holding back tears stared back at him. Lucas had not had a smooth relationship with his grandmother, in part because she always asserted that she did not have any patience for small children and in part because his own parents did not encourage it. When the little boy began to explore the mysteries of love,

"Mom, do you love me? Do you love Dad? And Grandmother, do you love her?" Sylvia lied-didn't-lie to the first two queries and her answer to the third just became clear this minute.

"Your grandmother fed me, clothed me and educated me. She said it was her duty as a mother. I am grateful to her."

Behind the gratitude, the entreaty, the desperation, the hate. Why didn't she love Laura? Sylvia tried hard to please her and her rewards were many: "*lazy,*" "*dirty,*" "*irresponsible,*" "*you don't deserve what I break my back to give you,*" "*go ahead and put on all the make-up you want, you look like a cheap whore,*" "*at this rate, you'll never graduate ,*" "*who would want to marry a freak like you?*"

Sylvia turned to her father, dissolving in tears. He consoled her, but did not defend her. He would not team up with her against Laura.

"You know how your mother is. She's always exploding about something, but she's not a bad person."

"Dad, don't you realize that to her I'm just a piece of garbage?"

"No, Sylvita, that's not right. She is worried about you. She's afraid things won't go well for you in life. She wants you to be the best."

"The best, like her, when every article of clothing or toy she ever bought me was just to show off what a good mother she was?"

"Now you're exaggerating. You're so like her!"

"I don't want to be like her! I don't want to be a monster . . ."

"Come on Sylvita, it's not like that. There'll come a time when you'll be grateful for what she does. And there is one thing, unfortunately, she's right about."

"No!"

"Yes. The way the world is now, being the daughter of divorced parents is a mark against you. No good Jewish family is going to accept you as a daughter-in-law. That's why she said you were a freak. And those Catholic cases your mother has surrounded herself with, they don't marry Jews, especially if they're not rich. So you see now. You're going to have to make your own way my little girl."

On Mother's Day 1985, Sylvia wrote a letter, which was replaced at the last minute by a bath towel . . . What use was it to give it to a nearly blind old woman, whose memory only retained the triumphs and important personages of the past? It's useless now, thought Sylvia. And she gave her the towel, a large one, with which to keep on covering up.

Lucas, in this imaginary dialogue-monologue that had begun when he entered the house, interpreted it as an act of decency.

"For just a moment there, Mom, you felt pity. In some way, despite everything, you loved her." He wanted to evoke Sylvia, closing his eyes to allow the image to form. It didn't work—what appeared instead was a puzzle impossible to put together.

SECOND LETTER

Dear Francisco:

In our fourth year we had a wonderful Literature professor. He was old, bald, and had a limp, and he became delirious with ecstasy over Romantic poetry and operas depicting great passions. He was an old bachelor and he was constantly in love. This volcano of the sonorous voice gave us the most sensible advice I've ever heard in my life.

'When you're dying of love for someone, say so. Write them a letter of fire and blood. Hold nothing back. Tell him he makes you tremble. Regale him with the most sublime and primitive that you hope to experience with him.

Then, place the letter in an envelope. Seal it—at this point our breath caught in our throats—and then mail it to yourselves. As time passes, you'll be happier you did not fan the flames of a fire whose burns would have left you permanently scarred.' The booing and hissing was unanimous. He, very serious, opened Les Fleurs du Mal and murmured, 'some of you will understand me sooner, others later, and some of you never will.'

And so, Francisco, I am writing to you, but addressing this to myself. Ever since the first postgraduate class—do you remember the course I called second-rate and it really was second rate?—I felt your eyes, the dark eyes of a Moor, sweeping over me, undressing me, caressing my breasts. I imagined your hands between my legs, and I felt a burning wave of anticipation rush over me, after which I was suddenly cold, so intensely cold it made me shiver. It took an enormous effort to concentrate on what I was saying and it was even more difficult to address the class, because I couldn't keep my gaze from losing itself in yours or my voice from following my gaze.

I left that first class in pieces. You remember how I said so curtly: 'Ask questions when you're a little deeper into the subject matter.'

I ran down the stairs to the Main Office of the postgraduate program and practically sprang upon Julia, the secretary:

'Get me out of there . . . I can't.'

She picked up the cigarettes that were falling out of the pack, lit one and placed it in my mouth.

'First of all, sit down and calm yourself,' she said, 'then you can explain where I have to get you out from and what it is you can't do.'

'The postgraduate course. I can't give it.' It wasn't my voice, or my style.

'Let's see, Ms. Meyer,' Julia must have perceived that I was about to have an attack of hysteria, so she decided to oblige me to be more formal. 'Let's recapitulate a little. This is not your first postgraduate course. You promised to do it. Give me a good reason to replace you and I'll think about it. But it will have to be very good reason. I'm listening.'

Francisco, I had a very good reason: you. I was getting married to someone else in a few weeks and I had suddenly discovered—whether it was requited or not—passion. I didn't want to have anything to do with it. I had seen in Inés the kind of destruction brought about by passion.

With Jaime I felt safe, but in order to go forward it was imperative I get you out of my sight—I was not at all sure I could keep my body from wanting you.

I lowered my head. I couldn't explain all this to Julia, I could hardly explain it to myself.

'So, problem solved,' with a palm on my shoulders she added confidently, 'It's pre-wedding jitters. Don't let them take over. We all go through it.'

During the course I experienced all of the agonies of the inferno. I argued with Jaime about everything, abused most everyone around me, and they all put up with me: like Julia, they believed I had those 'special' nerves.

On the last day, when you came up and asked me to dinner, I wanted to yell yes, have dinner, make love, feel alive. But the violence of being so out of control terrified me. I felt, first and foremost, afraid of myself, ashamed at my lack of shame, self-conscious about your reaction, guilty on account of Jaime.

But I could not deprive myself of the chance to see you, one last time I supposed, and I suggested the café.

On autopilot, I explained what you probably knew better than I did, and I drank in your eyes, your hands, your mouth, your velvety voice.

I felt as if we were both experiencing the same thing. I couldn't marry someone else . . . if I'd only waited . . . but maybe we'd never have met . . . and how much more pain could I withstand, overcome with panic that it was just a passing thing, that you'd fall in love with someone else, someone pretty and happy, a mistress of artifice and seduction.

I was a coward. I married Jaime, expecting him to shelter me from the others, and especially from myself. I think that was the beginning of my anger at him: he not only did not protect me, but he couldn't see the ghost of the other—your ghost. I was sure you would not call me. I know very well that I forced you to work with me, and it was unfair to want you for myself from time to time, measuring the distance so you wouldn't get any closer than I could tolerate without abandoning my own rules by the wayside.

There is no way to find out, but maybe, just maybe, even if it was only for an instant, having you might have swept aside this deadly shadow that accompanies me and to which I will succumb so that in consuming me it will free me. Or perhaps I would have enshrouded you in my own darkness and I would never have forgiven myself for that.

Lucas was astounded. He could easily associate his mother with all sorts of negative passions. They had been her daily bread. But his mom had had the hots for that imbecile in her office? For years? *"What have you done, Ma? How did you always find a way to screw yourself? Why didn't you try it out, before, after, during? I thought you were brave. You said you had the world at your feet, until the world kicked your feet out from under you. I think one hemisphere of the world that really fucked you up was Grandmother Laura, even though you fought her, but at what cost, Ma? And the other was running into this guy, and then you couldn't stand up for yourself anymore. You'd gotten used to defending yourself on your own. You stuck the dagger in your heart before they could stick it to you first. How you must have hated yourself! And you never asked forgiveness. Remember you taught me NEVER to ask forgiveness? You said it was an attitude for beggars. How much fear, Mom, underneath the cocksure manner that made one want to slam you into a wall? 'If you believe, it exists,' you told me. I think maybe you loved me, a lot, and you were afraid that I'd love you so much I wouldn't be able to save myself from the darkness that engulfed you, afraid you'd infect me with the shadow of death that materialized next to your crib, calling you, tempting you, until you finally said, yes, "I want to." Now I know which deaths preceded you and who the dead were you supposedly had to replace. Poor Mom, the shadow didn't permit you to see the living.*

He balled up the letter and threw it into the wastebasket. That way he was sure it would not get mixed up with other papers that might unintentionally find their way into his father's hands. Sylvia's suffering was enough, along with his own, which was slowly welling up in him.

Francisco had barely gotten himself moved into the office when female phone calls began to rain down on him, purring, timid, impertinent.

Sylvia tried to sound him out, but his responses were clipped and the upshot always was, "It isn't anyone important."

Some came looking for him in the late afternoon. They were all pretty, professional, possessive. There were plenty who, hoping to ingratiate themselves with her, attempted various versions of *"Francisco has told me so much about you!"* Sylvia did not answer, always limiting herself to a neutral, "Wait for him a moment in the reception area." And she shut herself in her office thinking "How many more are going to parade through here?"

He was totally inconsiderate in his treatment of them. He left them standing on street corners when he finished up late and figured they'd have left by then, forgot dates they organized to introduce him to their friends. Sylvia was intrigued at how, the harsher the rebuff, the more they came back for more, until he, without preamble, took one last phone call and, without seeming to care whether or not she could hear—or perhaps precisely because she was in earshot—he'd cut off the relationship and the call.

"I'm not interested in seeing you again."

Sylvia often wondered what kind of husband he'd have been. When the passion was over, the bodily hunger sated, would she have found herself with a tyrannical, dominant, or indifferent being? A yes from deep within her reaffirmed that she'd been prudent in not allowing herself to be carried away by the most primitive, even if it was adorned with admiration and intelligence.

Throughout her desolate childhood and adolescence, she had concocted an ideal man: a sort of knight errant, attentive to her desires, a shield to protect her from life's misfortunes: a man with no chinks in his armor. Father and husband in that order. Or maybe mother and husband. Jaime had played both roles for a time. She had played the matching part of wife, for a time. One day she'd woken to Jaime's chinks. One here, another over there had transformed the structure she'd believed solid, the man from her fantasy, into a bundle of weaknesses that endangered the entire family but above all, plunged her into a well of panic in which the most mundane things could destroy her.

Even with the aid of sleeping pills, she spent entire nights awake, her heart exploding in her chest and a feeling of impending disaster she could not explain. She invoked it without naming it. The morning found her with circles under her eyes, listless, with the self-imposed obligation to confront the nausea that welled up in her uncontrollably, barely leaving her time to get to the bathroom.

Jaime sympathized at first, then became inured to it.

"Try to take refuge in your internal pasture," he told her more than once.

Sylvia stared at him blankly. She didn't have an internal pasture.

Inside, she was a barren expanse that offered no shelter from the threatening and brutal outside world.

"What is it that terrifies you so?" Garnet had inquired.

"Everything."

But just as her mother had, he probed and pressured.

" 'Everything' is too vague. Say it, one by one, what things."

"The voices. The sounds. The traffic. The people," and she cried until the words became unintelligible.

"Cry. Does it help?"

"No. I never cry," responded Sylvia between sobs.

"And yet you are crying now," he pointed out.

"Yes."

"Why are you crying, Sylvia?"

Silence. Minutes. Absences.

"It's not why it's for whom. I'm crying for myself, for the little girl I was, am. The little girl who never grew up, who tried to find her place in the world by faking adulthood, security, independence—a little bear among hungry wolves."

"So what do you think?"

"I don't know. It's just blank . . ."

"That's what you would like to believe . . . in a blank expanse where you could stay forever. Think about it."

THIRD LETTER

To Sylvia:

Lucas flinched. He didn't recall his mother having a friend by the same name. Who could it be? Well, if he succeeded in finding out who this Sylvia was, perhaps by asking his father, it would probably be appropriate to give it to her. But first, he had to read it.

Just to remember: I am completely responsible for what happens, and for having gotten to this point. I didn't see the warning signs in time. I lied to myself so much—'if you believe, it exists.' I was so convincing I swallowed my own lies like jam; sweet lies covering up so much shit, until the shit overflowed like a waterfall and I got sick. From depression, said the worthy doctor. From hate, I'd say. Hating myself, I hated them. As I sunk, I brought them down with me. But naturally, I keep up appearances: I work like a beast of burden and above all, outside of these walls, I keep on lying.

He speaks the truth: a) there isn't any, b) I don't have any, in any order.

In ten years we'll be begging in the streets.

If I don't get up the courage to put an end to this, I can envision an old age of insanity: the cracks are already visible, although he prefers not to look. It is apparent in the flashes of forgetfulness, the mental labyrinths in which I become increasingly lost, in the indifference whose flip side is the hate chipping away at me. I'll tell you-me once and for all Sylvia, the specter of physical decay, misery, and intellectual deterioration terrifies me. I can't overcome the exhaustion of pretending to be someone else, or the despair, or the certainty that if everything is very bad now, soon it will be a lot worse. The whole world lied to me and to my entire generation. It was all about, your education, your job, your retirement. And I, like a two-bit Cassandra, kept saying "It's not true." I didn't have any reason for saying it, apart from ' if you don't believe, it doesn't exist.' They threw every garland my way: incorrigible, pessimistic, wet blanket, defeatist, and public enemy. Like when I didn't celebrate the invasion of the Malvinas with that mob of idiots. And see what happened in the end? The idiots trained their accusatory looks on me: we'd lost the war only because I had taken it upon myself to think it.

I am overcome by hate. I cannot distinguish between my anguish and whatever it is they call life, as they go along unknowingly—not wanting to know—traipsing along the path, more or less disguised, more or less illusory, toward their own death. It is not a very original notion, but everyone around me is so ensconced in life, with their airs of immortality that, I repeat, I am overcome by hate. No. I promised you the truth: the hate is born out of my envy towards them.

Sylvia had written herself a letter to say . . . what? Lucas felt as if he could see her, disheveled, beside herself, screaming out her hate, her solitude, her contempt, her terrors. . . . It never would have occurred to him she was envious. And yet, when you really looked at it, she'd felt so deprived, so empty, so beggarly, that she could easily be envious, starting with the very breath of life he took for granted.

"I am exhausted," was her greeting upon returning home. "a creature of your making," said the letter to Grandmother Laura. Could it be that once upon a time she had actually been made? And he? Could it be that he was defective too and simply had not realized it?

He decided he needed to talk to Sylvia's friends, and also to his father.

The story he'd refused to hear from the primary source, would have to be told by others, deformed, subjective, whatever.

There was one last letter. It was addressed to Jaime and dated the year of their separation.

Lucas wavered briefly and then decided that one way or another, everything remaining in his house—it was his house now—belonged to him. He had a right.

He thought, as he unfolded it, *"Go ahead, keep on tying yourself up in knots, just like her. But she was your mother—you must have something in common, like it or not."*

Jaime:

I deceived you. Not with another man, although I had fantasies about someone, but you were so far from being jealous that even if you'd seen me in bed with another you'd have thought you were hallucinating. I fantasized, but at the center of my fantasy was the other-me, pretty, happy, carefree, giving and receiving love.

I deceived you when we met at the Christmas cocktail party hosted by your bank, remember?

As a bank attorney, I had on my social mask and I didn't take it off for a second, until Lucas was born, at least. I would say that even then I didn't take it off, but he, with his cries and his little hands, yanked it right off my face. After that, I could only wear it outside of the house.

I don't know if I loved you, or if I love you. I repeat that I don't know what it is to love: the term and its manifestations are foreign to me. They are the patrimony of the privileged.

I only told you my true history—or parts of it—after we'd been married for years. And my true history, devoid of the lies I had draped over it for myself, was hard. You never quite understood just how hard: ultimately I had never been battered, abused, or neglected by my family. I had never been seriously ill, I had not been through an abortion, there had been no drugs, no lunatics, no criminals in the picture.

That's how you understood it from your black and white dichotomy. I did not go out of my way to make you see how those colors fused into a gray that encompassed everything more subtly than your imagination was able to glimpse. I do realize I needed you, I still do and I guess I will as long as I live.

But I did not tell you that: I let you believe I could do it alone, while you disintegrated in the catastrophe of your stubbornness, your willfulness.

You founder all over the place, yet I still need you. More than once, unbeknownst to you, you protected me from myself in your own way. Maybe I resented the bridges you kept laying to keep me from falling into the abyss.

I am aware of how I hurt you, judging you pitilessly, leaving you out in the cold, shut out of my life when it was your turn to need shelter. But you know what? Deep down it was an act of generosity. I, who am selfish, could see which direction things were going and I didn't want you to be there when the moment came, tomorrow, in a few months, years maybe.

I understand that you don't know what to do with me when the insanity overcomes me. I know I scare you—I scare myself with my own violence!

I firmly believe that without me you'll move on. You'll be able to form a genuine relationship, not the poor imitation—my fault—that ours was.

I asked you to leave and it was terrible to watch you go. But what else could I do? You still retained some instinct for self-preservation, which I lack. In search of my death, I killed your happiness, your hope, your manhood. Now you have the chance to get them back. I hope you succeed.

Sylvia

The tears rolled down Lucas' cheeks. *She only mentioned me once. There's no room for me in her mind, but Dad, whose life she tore apart just like mine, deserves to be happy after all. She justifies it, restores to him the place she threw him out of so he wouldn't have to deal with what was coming, and what about me? I was the one who found her and she knew, she dedicated it to me. Oh Mom, why did you have to do it that way, why didn't you take care of me like when I was little? I remember moments, I remember when you were mean, perverse, crazy, vengeful, affectionate, concerned, hurtful, destructive, and who am I then, and for what am I?* Guttural sounds, uncontrollable sobs now came along with the certainty that he was an orphan of long standing, though his status had been covered up by two cardboard figures he'd called mom and dad.

"This letter I will deliver," he decided, when he was able to compose himself. "I guess."

"It'll probably just bring him down even more," remarked Estela later, after the church where he'd deposited the bags of Sylvia's clothes and belongings.

"Well, I can't divine the future. Let it be God's will then."

"And the collections of books and papers, Lucky? Did you give them away too?"

"I tossed the papers without looking at them, except for receipts and such. The books are there. I'm going to offer them to Francisco."

"But wasn't it that she didn't want anyone to have her things, or am I confused? Were the books separate?"

"I don't give a shit what she wanted. I'm not going to keep them. And throwing out books seems like sacrilege to me. If Francisco doesn't accept them, I'll give them away in the street."

Chapter IX

FACE TO FACE

Lucky's call took him by surprise. He didn't get along with him and it was mutual. Even so, he'd suggested he come by the office to talk. It suddenly dawned on him that the office was Lucas' property.

Whether he stayed or had to look elsewhere depended on the whim of the spoiled brat who'd never shown any interest in his mother's work. He'd show up once in a while announcing the reason for his visit from the doorway.

"Is my Mom here? I need some cash."

It made Francisco's stomach turn. He took advantage of the occasions in which Sylvia was out, or hadn't yet arrived, to inform him stonily:

"There isn't a dime in the petty cash box"—and he would regard Lucas provokingly, as if to encourage him, come on, I dare you to ask me. He imagined Lucas would eventually take the bait and then he'd have a golden opportunity to confront him with his indifference toward Sylvia, his negligence, not even coming with the car to get her when it was raining, and so on and so forth. What's known as a good talking to, from which the other would depart with his tail between his legs like a beaten dog.

He'd been left hanging. Without fail, Lucas had responded, "okay, I'll come back later on."

Sometimes he'd come back; other times he'd disappear for weeks on end.

He had never witnessed the conversations between mother and son, which generally lasted only a few minutes. Lucas would leave like someone who'd just wrapped up a transaction, and Sylvia would remain silent, absorbed in her thoughts for a long while, impervious to the ring of the telephone, the impatient shouts from the hallway calling for the elevator. Impervious to him, whom she'd stare at without seeing.

"Hey Sylvia, where are you?" Francisco would snap his fingers in front of her eyes.

"Did you have a problem with Lucas?"

She'd simply shake her head and change the subject.

"Pass me the Henríquez file please."

Clearly the spoiled brat was coming to claim what was his. It was his prerogative.

Lucas arrived at five o'clock on a Friday afternoon, two months after Sylvia's death.

In the crude fluorescent light of the little conference room his skin, drawn taut across his cheeks, appeared translucent.

"*He looks like a goblet on the verge of cracking,*" thought Francisco as they sat down across from each other.

With his lost gaze, Lucas looked so much like Sylvia! He did not speak. Arms crossed, knees drawn against his chest, he called to mind an ice sculpture.

The minutes passed. Francisco waited patiently: he did not want to be the one to make the first move.

When Lucas was ready, he fired.

"I know you can't stand me."

He cut short Francisco's protest with a wave of his palm.

"Wait. Let me speak. You think I was a bad son. You think I didn't deserve the mother I had, etc. etc. It's true, I didn't deserve her, but not in the way you think. You were acquainted with Ms. Meyer the attorney, not with my old lady. I have no intention of spelling out the difference for you. She's dead and that's it. I've come to ask you whether you would like her library. Are you interested?"

"Why give it to me?" Francisco was more than willing to accept. They were books Sylvia had read, reread, marked up, underlining and noting her comments in the margins. It would be like having her, her thoughts, her words. But he couldn't understand the motive behind Lucas' generosity. Why hand over such a treasure to someone who—truth be told—couldn't stand him? "Don't you want to keep them? They were very important to your Mother . . . an important part of her life . . ."

"Sure. Much more important than the people."

"What?"

"Don't mind me. Stupidities. I don't read that sort of books and I don't like seeing them around. It doesn't matter why. Do you want them or not?"

"Of course I do. When can I go pick them up?"

"No, I'll have them delivered to you. Here or at your home?"

"Well, I've been meaning to ask you what is going to happen with the office. Are you planning to sell it or rent it?"

"I don't know yet. I'm in no rush. You can stay, taking over the expenses, until I decide what to do. I suppose you'll be taking over the cases my mother left pending . . ."

Francisco's face twisted into a strange expression. Lucas didn't know? At this point there was no choice but to tell him.

"Sylvia had no cases pending."

"Don't tell me she carefully wrapped everything up before she killed herself?"

So it was true! Francisco evoked the conversation with Inés and Clara in the phantasmagoric atmosphere of the funeral parlor. Then he'd asserted it as if he'd had hard evidence. Yet as the days passed his certainty had begun to crumble to the point where he'd regretted his words. He had considered calling his companions of that vigil to tell them he'd been carried away by despair, that his imagination had clouded his thinking in his desire to explain the intolerable and they should just forget it. Finally he had decided not to reopen the matter. They would take responsibility for their own suspicions and he would eventually allow himself to be persuaded that Sylvia wasn't capable of . . . But the little brat had tossed it out in such an offhand way! He wasn't about to let it pass just like that.

"What are you saying, Lucas? Two months ago it was a heart attack. Now it turns out it was suicide?" His voice hardened; he was setting himself up as both judge and jury.

"At the time, Dad didn't want it known. He fixed it so—" he shrugged. "You know how it is. In this country you can fix anything. It no longer matters. It's all the same. The outcome I mean. So, going back, you say she finished everything up beforehand?"

"Sylvia had no cases pending because . . . she hadn't had any cases for quite a while."

"What do you mean she didn't have any cases?" Lucas could not contain his astonishment. His mother had been incredibly busy up to the last day. Or was it another lie? *If you believe, it exists.*

"Over that last year, she'd begun to lose clients . . . some said she was slow, as if distracted. Others complained she was too expensive, out of sync with the economic reality. And new clients—well they just didn't materialize. You know it all operates based on referrals."

"That's what happened? You saw it?"

"Yes. She lost interest; she didn't care if she missed a deadline, didn't keep track of the files. It was as if they . . . turned her off, documents and clients. And she didn't lower her rates either."

"So the clients switched over to you?" Lucas' question came across like a statement: *You took advantage of my mother.*

"Don't think badly of me. I would never have taken a case from your mother, unless she specifically asked me to. Some came to me, it's true, looking around. '*Mr. Rossi, weelll . . . it looks as if Ms. Meyer isn't quite keeping up. Couldn't you take over my case in the mean-*

time?' You have no idea how hard I tried to get Sylvia to get moving. But she didn't care. It was like she wasn't there. She encouraged me to take the cases; I didn't want to. So she started referring them to other colleagues, in a way that was clearly saying, *'I'm done—with you, with your case and with whatever happens to you from here on out.'* This did not go over well as you might imagine."

True to form. In this outward explosion, Lucas recognized the pattern of behavior Sylvia had kept hidden within the four walls of home.

"There's something I don't get, Francisco. If she went for a year without working, what were we living on?"

"From legal fees owed to her that were being paid in; from savings I guess. I have no idea how she managed her money."

Lucas was on the verge of opening up, then stopped himself. It was much too private to discuss with this guy.

"Well then, here or your house?"

"What?"

"The books."

"Oh, yes. My house. I'm not sure whether I'm going to stay here, although I do appreciate the offer."

He noted the address on a card adding, "I'll let the doorman know to let them in. He has a key, so send them whenever you want."

He accompanied Lucas to the door. They shook hands and Lucas waited for the elevator. He felt too weak to take the stairs as usual.

Francisco tried to concentrate on the document he was drafting. Hopeless. The questions whirled around in his head; answers were not forthcoming. Why had Sylvia hidden from her son the fact that she had stopped working? For that matter, why stop working if you didn't have any means of support? Did it have to do with gradually letting go of the things she felt tied her down in preparation for the final release? But why? Why hadn't she let herself receive help, real help, through love, not the pompous psychiatrist whose voice on the telephone—the few times he'd called at the office—had been enough to know he was incompetent. Why, Sylvia? Why?

Jaime arrived about an hour late at the bar where he'd told Lucas to meet him. It was a cheap, rundown place near San Juan and Boedo, with tables balanced on uneven legs and a mixture of ill-defined odors, sliced with whiffs of body odor. Jaime had selected it because it was cheap; for Lucas it was also clear he was a "regular:"

the Spanish immigrant behind the counter had asked him if he was Don Galván's son, commenting, "You can't imagine how proud your father is of you. Have a seat boy, over there. That's his table. Get whatever you like, eh."

"Hello, son. I had no idea it was getting so late. But I had to go over to . . . and the train . . . so before . . ."

Lucas had switched off. True to form.

"No problem. I had stuff to read."

"Have you ordered?" inquired Jaime signaling the waiter.

"No, a Coke," he said in the direction of the raised eyebrows. The guy didn't even bother to ask; wouldn't want to waste his breath.

"Coffee for me," said Jaime, taking out cigarettes, lighter, glasses, agenda, as if he were planning to stay a good while.

"Dad, I have something to give you that I found among Mom's papers. I'm going to ask you not to read it right now. Could you do that?"

"Did you read it?"

"Yes, because it was open; I've put it in an envelope; it's a letter for you."

"And if you knew it was for me, don't you think maybe you shouldn't have read it?"

"Dad, given the way Mom left it, I don't think she really cared who read it."

"What does it say?"

"You'll see when you read it. It's painful . . . that's why I'd prefer you to read it later, okay?"

"Fine," Jaime placed the envelope in his agenda book. "I've hardly seen you at all these last few months . . . I had the feeling you were . . . escaping?"

"No . . . yes, well maybe . . . It's just that I wanted to talk to you about Mom; Or rather, I wanted you tell me about Mom, but at the same time it hurt a lot, you know? Now isn't the time either . . . this place . . . her hair would've stood on end seeing us here."

Jaime's gaze swept over the other customers: faces marked by hardship or absorbed in past losses; lines of despair, resignation, used up faces, regardless of age. His was probably indistinguishable from theirs; he knew it and accepted it. Lucas' was out of place; he still had a lot ahead of him.

"Would this weekend work for you? I'll meet you wherever you like, but remember . . ."

86

". . . I don't have any money," chimed in Lucas. "We don't have to spend anything. I'll pick you up on Saturday at three and we'll go to Lezama Park."

"That's where your mother and I used to take you when you got your first scooter. Remember?"

"Sort of."

"Well, you were pretty little."

"I don't know if it was that I was so little. The fact is, I don't remember a lot of things. That's why I need to talk to you. So you can help me remember, and so you can tell me."

In the bright afternoon sun the state of deterioration of the park saddened them both. Thin grass with huge bald patches, garbage everywhere, the intermingled cries of adults and children, broken down benches.

"Was it like this when we used to come here?" Lucas wanted to know. For him the place was so unfamiliar it was as if he'd never set foot here.

Jaime answered with another question.

"What made you think to come here?"

"I don't know. It was the first place that came to mind."

"Well, it was always pretty neglected, but it was close by and there was this hill, see? Perfect for toy cars and scooters. Mom would unfold her lawn chair in the sun and I'd help you get ready to take off and then run down the hill to wait for you. When you starting riding your bike more, we'd go to the KDT track in Palermo, and then to the go-kart track at the Automobile Club, and we'd have picnics in Escobar, and take boat rides at el Tigre . . . Do you remember, Lucky?"

"I see myself . . . as if it's not me, you know?"

"And yet you had a great time with all of it. We called you the good time boy."

"I can see you carrying the scooter, and biking with me. But it's as if Mom wasn't there . . ."

Jaime's eyes clouded, lost in the images of the posthumous letter, Sylvia merging into the images of countless other Sylvias who still called out to him during the sleepless nights.

"Mom . . . was there when she was able. She often didn't feel well. So then you and I would go, just the two of us."

"Like when we started going to the club . . ."

"By that time your Mom was very sick."

"You say it as if she'd had a terminal illness," resisted Lucas. "She just didn't want to put herself out. She was selfish; she said so herself."

"Oh Lucky." Jaime signed deeply, scraping the bottom of the eternity that was the past. "She said it so often we believed her. She even fooled herself. You have to look at it from another perspective."

"Yeah, sure. From outside the grave. And she doesn't even have a grave."

Lucas' bitterness cast a pall over the sun. The park—regardless of its condition it was still a park—was vanishing into a fog of a pain that was sweeping away the saving relief of those first days without Sylvia.

"Dad, tell me please." The question came out in a child's voice from the mouth of a twenty-year-old man."

Jaime didn't ask what he wanted to know. He started to talk, maybe for Lucas, maybe for himself, crafting a story. He wasn't sure whether or not it was the true story, but it truly was the one he believed.

SYLVIA THROUGH JAIME

When I met your Mom I was quite a looker—don't laugh, it's true. And the ladies were all over me like flies. And I paid court to all of them and to none. There was definitely room in my plans for the ladies, just not for *one* lady. Your mom was very pretty; yes, although you can't imagine her that way: she had fantastic legs and a figure to match, in her very slender style. She had beautiful eyes and an expressive, animated expression, and long, straight hair the color of mahogany that was brushed to the left side and hung below her shoulders to the middle of her chest. And you know what? She didn't bite like the others. I had to go after her. I fell in love straight away and the more time I spent with her the more convinced I became that I wanted to be with her for the rest of my life. She was so funny, with such a peculiar sense of humor that she made me laugh even when something was sad. Don't look at me like that, like I'm making up a fairy tale for you. *That's how it was.* And I was in a big hurry to get married. I was afraid someone else would come along and sweep her away, since she was always surrounded by men, because of her profession, and a couple of them were after her. And since I'm supposed to be telling you the truth, I was afraid one fine day she would wake up wondering, *"What am I doing with this guy?"* Because every single one of those fools who didn't take out their Ph.Ds even to pee were smooth talkers, they could confuse anyone if they really wanted to; professional de-formation, nothing like me. So I took the plunge and she said yes and we were all very happy . . . with a few exceptions. For instance? For instance, your grandmother Laura, who had hoped to dazzle her circle with a powerful and rich son-in-law. Or my parents, who were not ready to accept a Jewish daughter-in-law. Your other grandfather? He'd already passed away, but he'd have been in total agreement with my parents: a Catholic son-in-law would be tantamount to the devil. But her friends and mine were delighted. Yes, you see? She had a lot of friends, men and women. She went out nearly every night, and when I started becoming part of the group, I felt as if I'd known them my entire life. They went back a long way and they loved bringing up the past, impersonating themselves, the whole bit. Those were very good years. Amidst the political horrors and economic downturns we were going through, our house was a refuge from which the outside world was excluded. You know, Lucky, that we didn't have a TV? We read, we talked, we cooked, we entertained, we sang. We loved to sing. Do you remember what Mom sang to you when you were little? *"I come from the white poplars, mother; from watching the wind make them sway . . ."* So why did it all go bad? I don't have an answer to that. It was gradual and I didn't want to face it; I guess I thought it wasn't serious, that she'd get over it. When you were born she was gripped by desperation, a tremendous anguish. No, it wasn't that she didn't love you—what did you say? She felt too weak to protect you; suddenly the world was full of dangers, enemies, including me. She tried to pull herself together lots of times, but then the breakdowns would be worse, longer, harder to get past. It got to the point when I didn't know whether we left her alone because we couldn't stand being with her, or whether she wanted to be alone and forced us to leave her so she could throw it in our faces later. It was an insane circle. I felt guilty over her, over you, and I took on the universal blame. I didn't have the balls to divvy up the score; I gave in to her and to you . . . What do you mean I didn't give you anything? Do you know how many times I should have said "no" to you? Yes, she said it, for both of us. She always said *no*, just in case, when her mind wasn't very clear. I know it was bewildering. But if you take the time to think it over the figure begins to take shape. And there is a certain volume that's made up of such contradictory forms you can't believe they're all part of the same person. I think at first, during those good years, she shoved her dark side way to the back, to the point that she forgot about it. Until the darkness began to creep insidiously into her bones, into her mind; and it began to manifest itself. And then she gave and held back, she loved and hated, she fought and conceded defeat, she was beautiful and horrible. After that she turned into a malignant and destructive being, from which the best you could expect was indifference because it meant she didn't even look at you and you were safe from attack. Ultimately she wanted to blow up the world and I think she realized the world was inside her. Don't ask me for the real reason, like you did when you were little. There were a lot of them I guess, or maybe there wasn't one. The only thing I can tell you in all honesty is that I loved her and I also hated her, and I never was able to grasp the atrocious suffering she was going through. My world is more concrete; hers was populated by ghosts. She herself, shuffling about the house in her nightdress, collapsed on the bed like a broken doll, dragging herself to work each morning, was the ghost of a Sylvia who might have been.

"Are you trying to tell me she did everything she could?"

"For as long as she was able, yes. It's getting chilly. Let's go; call Estela and I'll make you some pasta with your favorite sauce."

"All right."

SYLVIA THROUGH INÉS

"Let's see, Lucky, put the plans on the floor and sit down anywhere you can."

"This apartment's getting too small for you. You have a lot of business, don't you?"

"Quite a bit. But it all comes in at once. Just now there's a surge in people remodeling those old mansions . . . What can I serve you?"

"Whatever you're drinking."

"*Mate.* Bitter."

"That's fine . . . Mom used to love mate, but she didn't know how to prepare the infusion. Strange, isn't it?"

Inés studied him openly. How much of Sylvia was there in Lucky? Nothing physically; he had his father's features and build. Perhaps some character trait: the firmness with which he had asked to see her "to talk about my mother."

"What's strange?"

"That you never learn how to prepare something you like and you have to depend on someone else, or go without."

"Mmm. But Sylvia was pretty lazy about certain things. Bah, I'm not sure whether it was laziness or whether she just considered them a waste of time. For example, she never wanted to learn how to light the coals for a barbecue. She said it was a man's job; and she couldn't sew on a button either. In your house, it was your dad who sewed, or the cleaning girl . . . Your mom was quite *machista* I'd say."

"If she was machista then I don't get the thing about the sewing."

"No, that was something different. There was an entire universe that did not interest her: sewing, knitting, mathematics, technology, the hole in the ozone, politics. As long as someone else was taking care of it, she'd just stick to her own things."

"But what does sewing have to do with politics?"

"Nothing, they just appear together on the same list summarizing the things your mom didn't give a damn about."

"I don't understand. In that salad, very manual things are mixed in with other very abstract ones. And yet she loved to cook, although toward the end she wouldn't even fry an egg."

Inés regarded him in amusement. The kid had not been very observant and no one had bothered to enlighten him.

"The kitchen was a ball breaker for Sylvia. As she sashayed around, a clean orderly place would become a pile of scum, grease, trash, stains, who knows what; it was completely out of control. But yes, she liked to eat good food, and so she made the sacrifice. Aside from that, she wanted you to get used to eating all kinds of food. She wasn't about to foist off hamburgers and hotdogs on you, like other mothers did. When she separated from your father and you were all grown up and all of a sudden you weren't going to be home for dinner, she didn't feel like cooking for herself, or cooking something that would just rot in the fridge day after day. Didn't you know that the refrigerator is just the dumpster's antechamber? You put stuff in there, you cling to the illusion it's going to last and if you wait too long, the smallest little fungus wouldn't fit in the palm of your hand.

"Inés! You may be from the day of the refrigerator but haven't you noticed those little gadgets they call freezers and microwaves? And that the fridge has a freezer attached?"

"No little barbs, eh! It's all well and good that I'm sort of an aunt to you, but you're not paying serious attention. What did I tell you about your mom and technology? She wasn't interested. I remember once when we spent the weekend in Colonia. I had gone out shopping. She wanted to heat up some tea in the microwave and ended up having to call the maid to show her how. The story was all over the hotel. Another mate?"

"I pass. You and Mom were very different weren't you?"

"Different and alike."

"In . . . ?"

"We both spent our lives struggling. Your mom's way, when we were young, was a passive, stubborn resistance. When she had no other choice but to talk, she'd cut you down in two sentences. Luckily, we were on the same side!"

"What do you mean spent your lives struggling? To me it makes it sound as if you had to earn the daily bread, but I know that wasn't the case."

Inés lit a cigarette and tried to conjure up the 1960s, the 1970s. Sylvia and she had not fought for the same things. But when it came down to it, all those details wouldn't add much as far as Lucky was concerned.

"Your mom struggled against her fears. Your grandmother Laura terrified her. Entering a room full of people, whether a classroom or a party, would cause her to fall apart. Traveling outside the country reduced her to panic. Being in a relationship with a man scared her to death. I could make you a list from here to eternity. And the more afraid she was, the more she insisted on confronting it."

"But what was she afraid of? I understand less and less."

"Haven't you ever been afraid, Lucky? Pure fear, for no specific reason?"

"Of course not. I'm not crazy."

"Sylvia wasn't either. But the fear is real and if your own mother digs the earth out from under your feet, a sinister question starts to take form: If I'm nothing but trash to her, then what am I really? I thought she'd overcome it . . . more recently I realized that she was the same . . . worse."

The immutable truth of the suicide hovered in the air. Neither of them uttered the word.

"Did Mom talk to you about what was going on with her?"

"She didn't want to talk. And when Sylvia didn't want to do something, there was no way around it."

Abruptly, Lucas let slip his own conclusion.

"Mom wasn't so different from grandmother Laura."

"You're totally mistaken about that. And you know what the proof is? You are free of the fear that tormented her."

92

"So Dad was just a stick of furniture?"

"What?"

"I'm saying, couldn't it be that Dad did what she couldn't?"

"Jaime did his part, yes. But don't you recall any good times with Sylvia?"

Not without effort, some of the high points began to come into his head; the games, the sketchbooks of little figures they'd done together, the cartoons they'd watched, the books she'd read to him until he'd gotten into the habit of reading, how she'd listened when he told her about his friends, or his little girlfriends . . . Terrible moments invaded too; they seemed to weigh so much more! But he nodded in silence. They had shared some good times.

"You see?" insisted Inés, "don't erase them. That was also your mom, capable of giving you those moments of security. I'm going to tell you something, but first I want you to answer a question. People you are introduced to, do they remember you when you run into them again?"

"Of course. Sometimes even people I've never been introduced to recognize me . . ."

"Good. When Sylvia began to work as an assistant in Public Law, the department chair was a very prominent lawyer, but he wasn't at all arrogant; he was friendly and considerate. A woman who had been her professor and had been promoted to deputy chair took your mom to see him. Dr. Maroni received them in his office, the two of them alone. Her prof had already told him about Sylvia; she formally introduced her, and they had an interview that lasted about forty minutes and concluded with Sylvia as his brand new assistant. Two weeks later the first department meeting is held. Maroni arrives last, greets the group, suddenly notices Sylvia seated among the others, and frowns. He calls his deputy chair aside and they whisper for a few seconds, but since the room had fallen into one of those total, uncomfortable silences, you could hear what they were saying. I'll make it brief: Maroni wanted to know who the girl at the meeting was. The deputy chair had to remind him about the interview, her name, and her position. "Ah yes, now we can begin," he murmured. But each time their paths crossed, sometimes Sylvia herself had to remind him again of who she was. And the same thing happened at parties, anywhere. "This girl" was the way your grandmother Laura had always referred to her. I never heard her refer to you as "this boy.""

"No she called me by my name or my nickname. But when she was really bad off she called me all sorts of things."

"It's something. At least it's a thousand times better than 'this boy.' As if she didn't know where he came from; a nameless being, a nothing."

"And if I wasn't a nothing, why did she leave me like this, with no word, no sign?"

"It seems to me there were a lot of signs, but you are too young to have seen them. I believe she thought the damage had reached the point of being intolerable, for her and for you. I'm not excusing it; I'm just trying to understand."

"She fucked up my life."

"Perhaps, for a time. But think about just how far you were willing to accompany her."

"She didn't let . . ."

"I know."

"She had no right!"

Inés heard the echo of Francisco's words, pronounced the night of the wake: "spoiled brat."

"You're wrong, although I doubt you'll accept it. Do you realize what kind of life your mother led?"

"The one she chose certainly. I never saw her do anything she didn't want to."

"*Like puppies,*" mused Inés, "*We were like that too.*"

"Lucky, let's see, make an inventory. What did Sylvia like to do?"

"Make our lives miserable, Dad's and mine."

"I'm serious. Did she like to go out? To the movies, the theater, get-togethers, for a walk, window shopping, to hear music?"

"She hated to go out. When she had no choice, and always because of a commitment, she'd bitch the whole day before and the day after as well. Music, zero. She didn't even have a radio. I'd say that what she most liked to do was throw herself down on the bed and watch TV. Anything on TV."

"And that's living?"

"It was to her."

"No, Lucky. When we were young, your mom went to the beauty parlor once a week; we went to the Colón, went out dancing and to art exhibits, we never missed a play or a good movie. We'd get together to discuss books. We went out nearly every night. We'd take off on weekend getaways whenever we could. And we studied. When I had stuff due, she'd come to the house to study and keep me company during those endless all-nighters. In the background we'd tune into the truckers' radio."

It seemed to Lucas as if she were talking about someone else. So, is this what she'd wanted to share with him and he'd refused to listen?

"Was that before she met Dad?" He suspected Jaime had been the bending point.

"Before and after . . . for a time."

"Do you know what happened; why she went to the other extreme?"

"No, I don't know. She started pulling away and we couldn't get her back. Not even your father . . . not that he made such a huge effort."

"That I don't accept. He was always bugging her to come with us."

"Bugging her wasn't a good idea. She did tell me that he never came to her with a plan in mind, just for the two of them. When someone organized something, Jaime would just go along passively. But a romantic surprise, an invitation to go dancing, a gift just because, all of that went up in smoke when you were born. It stung her . . . until she stopped caring."

"So I was the obstacle then?"

"No, no. But your father was very attached to you. He couldn't conceive of outings that didn't include you. I'm not criticizing him; it's a description of the situation, that's all."

"But she could have made plans elsewhere, or she could have made plans like the ones you were talking about—," Lucas was stubbornly trying to find solutions that might have changed the course of events.

"Could have, but she wasn't capable of it. Whenever we went out somewhere we always had to give her a little push. A positive push, not bug her. There was something . . . I don't know what it was, that was missing in her. The attachment to silly little things that make you happy for a moment. You had to give her a lot of line and watch out for when it was about to run out."

"And Dad didn't know that?"

"I think she didn't allow him to know and if he realized it at some point, it was already too late for both of them. Well then, do you feel better?"

"I feel strange. I need to process it all, Inés. Everything you've said sounds contradictory to me and it's sort of the opposite of what my Dad told me, and it has no correlation to what I experienced at home . . . I get the feeling we all think we're talking about Mom, but we're really talking about different people."

"It makes sense. We all speak based on the Sylvia we knew, and based on what she wanted us to see, or to guess, or whatever. Don't be a stranger; come over and bring Estela whenever you like."

SYLVIA THROUGH SILVINA

"Get me a glass of water and a couple of aspirins, will you? My head is about to explode," Silvina asked her eldest daughter, aged 27. Lucas had just left and Silvina collapsed on the sofa, cursing the moment of weakness that had prevented her from finding an excuse not to see him.

"Did Lucas make your head spin?" inquired Claudia, laughing, "or did you talk so much you made your own head spin? Because I didn't hear much out of him . . ."

"You were listening?"

"No Ma! I was in my room, with the door ajar, and this apartment is like a palace of echoes . . . I'll be right back."

Silvina lay back on the sofa and closed her eyes. She felt drained, as if those memories she'd picked apart for Lucas were no longer part of her.

Grimacing at the bitter taste (just of the aspirins?) she swallowed the pills and asked Claudia to leave her alone for a while. She wanted to go over the story again mentally, to try to recover her Sylvia, the Sylvia of her childhood, of the words of wisdom. She wished desperately to erase the vision of the final Sylvia, the one that, according to Lucas, had given herself over to death with what she imagined to have been a terrifying indifference.

How to begin, for herself this time?

Once upon a time . . . there once was a girl in kindergarten. She was serious, so much so she seemed to be a miniature grown up lady. She was always asking permission: to eat a cookie, to leave the table; she always said thank you. She often refused to join in the childish mischief that Silvina and their other little friends delighted in "because my mom doesn't let me."

"But your mom isn't here!"

"She still doesn't let me."

Silvina was aware that her own mother, visiting with her woman friends at their afternoon get-togethers, gossiped animatedly (in very low voices of course) and amidst the murmurs she could distinguish the name "Sylvita." Silvina imagined those moms were consumed with admiration for her best friend and that the reason for all the whispering was that they didn't want their own daughters to get jealous.

Throughout her childhood, Sylvita was the queen of the birthday parties. With her exquisite frocks, matching shoes and lace stockings, she was in charge of reciting beautiful poems that brought tears to the eyes of children and adults alike.

I with my own hands have dug the hole
I with my own hands the cedar sowed.

How did it go? Something she couldn't remember and then another line:

The cedar will be young and I'll be old.

It was easy to see she studied recitation with the best teacher! It seemed as if her soul went into each word, each gesture . . . Ah yes. The forgotten line found its way back into the stanza and Silvina started over, aloud, but it wasn't the same; the magic had been in Sylvia's voice, not the verses.

"I with my own hands have dug the hole.

"I with my own hands the cedar sowed.

"And years upon years shall pass by,

"And the cedar will be young and I'll be old."

So sad, my God! Always so sad. But then would come the fun, the balloons, the circle games; the memory of the poem would fade and the songs, the laughter, the chocolate would remain. And Sylvia standing in a corner, lost, forgotten, sometimes (but only sometimes) rescued by Silvina and dragged into the vortex of the pure pleasure of being a little girl.

At school, others were selected to recite during the patriotic holidays after the first time when Sylvia, standing on the immense stage of the auditorium, had forgotten the lines of an extremely long poem about the seasons. She had been navigating anxiously through summer and fall, but when it was Mr. Winter's turn, she'd spread her arms open like a cross and, as if waking from an enchantment, had shouted, "Mom, I don't remember!" Curtain and applause. The mother approached, understanding, but had shoved her about a little—or had Silvina inserted that part as she recalled the scene? In any case, there was a formal request from the Regent that there be no repeat of a situation which might *"expose her to humiliation in front of other people, not to mention her own classmates."*

And even so, she was always the one chosen to tell stories.

During a long bout with the measles, her father had given her a book of Greek mythology.

"What an idea, filling a child's head with such things," was Laura's commentary.

But they had given her permission to read it, a permission that Sylvia extended to telling those marvelous stories to her friends. Overheard by a teacher, soon they were fighting over her during the free periods of all the grades, even the secondary section. She, a little girl, was capable of inspiring a captivated silence toward those lost worlds.

"How can you remember so many names and all those complicated plots?" Silvina had asked a short time before her attention would be distracted by those other marvelous and mythical beings: boys.

"It's like remembering the names of your relatives . . . The plots are more or less the same as in any large family."

"But the monsters? Are you going to tell me that's the same?"

"Almost . . . although we don't get to see their true faces."

That Sylvia! Already "philosophizing."

Pausing for a moment in her rosary of memories, Silvina smiled at the thought. She'd always labeled anything intangible "philosophy," or anything that obliged her to double check whether she really understood it. Maybe that was why she'd admired Sylvia so: even as a little girl, she talked complicated.

Where was she? Ah yes. Boys. In those days the schools weren't coed and contact with boys one's own age was limited to brothers and cousins, if one had any that is. But they moved in other circles where girls were, sometimes, tolerated.

Once they turned fourteen or fifteen, however, the idea was that both sexes would socialize at dances organized in "family homes." The transition was not hard for Silvina. Guided by her cousins and her cousins' friends, and with the advantage of being pretty and funny, she danced from the moment she arrived until the owners of the house shut down the party.

It was, for Sylvia, a painful lesson: she had to learn to make empty conversation, to understand the flirtation and play along, to follow the dance steps in fashion and to smile, to seem fun, docile, lovable, to not be relegated by the other boys and girls under the label of "no, not that drip, please." The phrase had hurt her ears when, early in her teens, she'd connected her telephone to Silvina's and paralyzed, unable to speak or hang up, she'd had to bear how Silvina stood up for her so they'd invite her to the party on Friday. When the other person hung up and there was no tone, Silvina had shaken the receiver.

"Hello! Hello!"

And she'd heard a voice she hardly recognized, so low, so defeated.

"Hello."

"Sylvita? But I didn't even hang up with . . ."

And it was then she realized.

"Sylvita, did you hear what we were saying?"

Silence.

"Sylvita, answer me. Did you hear it, yes or no?"

"Yes."

"Sylvita, they don't understand . . . that you . . . are interested in more important things . . . that . . ."

"They understand perfectly well that I'm a drip."

"No, no. You're different, deeper."

"A drip."

"Sylvita, please! Did you hear me say that?"

"I heard you defend me, ask on my behalf like for a beggar. And you know what? it would be good if it were different, if it didn't bother me. Deep down I feel like they're all a bunch of cretins, but I still want to be like them, like all of you. I want to be happy about the dresses my mom makes for me, one for each party, know the words to all the popular songs, feel that special look the boys caress the other girls with. I don't want them to pity me!" And then the heartrending sobs.

"Don't cry Sylvita. Everything's going to be all right. I'll help you, you'll see. But you have to change a little. I'm coming over to your house. We'll start right now."

Finally it had worked . . . to a point.

Now, the charade over, Silvina started to feel guilty. What good had she done Sylvia by fabricating that social life, the repartee?

Openmouthed, Lucas had asked her:

"But she knew which was the real her? Or did it make her sick to leave the house as one type of person and return home another?"

"Don't worry, Lucky. She was never ever confused. I do know she would have liked the 'fake' way of being, if you will, to become the real one. She deceived me. Well, I'm not very perceptive. I was excited to think the tricks had worked; above all, she had boyfriends, she was received, she married, she had you . . ."

"Did she ever tell you why she never had any other children? You, your friends, have several . . ."

"Except for Clara, who has none, yes."

"You're not answering my question, Silvina."

"It's that I'm not sure. We spoke about it many times. Sylvia was putting it off. . . ."

"But she couldn't stand putting things off!"

"Well, there are things and then there are things. Some decisions take more time. Am I mistaken or did you not have a tantrum every time a little brother or sister was mentioned?"

"It's true. I didn't want to share Mom and Dad with anyone else. Like any only child, right? Until the next one arrives and you don't die and you don't kill it."

"It was more important to her what you were going to go through."

"Come on, Silvina; if Mom gave a damn what I might go through. If she'd cared one whit . . ."

"That's enough Lucky. What we don't know we're not going to make up. You're going to have to be satisfied with 'because she didn't.' "

He had gone around and around a couple more times, still not convinced that this particular source had dried up. She felt badly that Sylvia had not had other kids. Without knowing how, something like a sign made up of neon tubes entered her head: TERRIBLE PARENTS. And the headache exploded in the shrapnel of the destroyed tubes, laying bare the blinding light of some truth.

SYLVIA THROUGH CLARA

"Clara, why don't you want to talk about Mom?"

Damned if the little brat wasn't direct. What to do? Keep making excuses or answer him, knowing that if he caught her with her guard down, she'd say more than she should? But if she kept avoiding him, he'd never leave her in peace. He was a bulldog just like his mother.

"Very well, Lucas. There are, however, three conditions."

"What is this, a game of forfeits?" Lucas wanted her to loosen up, this woman who was so much older than Sylvia, and so much sharper too.

"I'm not joking. First of all, I'm not going to answer any questions."

"But then . . ."

"Don't interrupt me. I'm not going to answer your questions, I'm not going to help you speculate about why your mother did or didn't do something, and I'm not going to listen to posthumous accusations. Understood?"

"No, but tell me anyway, where shall I meet you?"

"At the zoo entrance. Sunday at noon.

"On Sunday at the zoo? You've got to be kidding."

"Shh. In front of the ticket booth. On time."

Clasping Estela's hand, Lucas forged a path among the teeming crowd that blocked access to the ticket booths. Few planned to actually go in; they couldn't afford it. So what were they doing there? A conditioned reflex perhaps. They automatically headed for a pretty spot that had once been in the public domain, before privatization. They fluttered about the confluence of avenues like moths hypnotized by the light. Through government after government whose common denominator had been to ignore them, the people had lost everything except the streets themselves.

"I don't get it," Estela commented, "What is the fun of spending hours milling around, looking through the bars?"

"Just to be there. We Argentines will settle for just being there," muttered Lucas. "And that's no small feat considering what we've been through. See if you can spot Clara."

"Lucky, you didn't tell her you were bringing me. What if she doesn't like it?"

"That's one condition she didn't impose on me."

It was evident from Lucas' wicked grin that he wasn't going to be docile with Clara. Estela smiled too. This was her Lucas.

Dark glasses and a gray wool hat, Clara approached them from behind, tickets in hand.

"We're going to have to buy one more," she said in a neutral tone.

"Does it bother you?" prodded Lucas.

"Not in the least."

"Ah, no. If you want to spar with me, Lucky, you'll need to have a lot in your corner. And even so, it remains to be seen whether I want to spar with you."

They walked in silence along the lake trail, until Clara proposed they sit on one of the old iron benches to observe the majestic passage of the swans, indifferent to the June cold or the human presence.

Impenetrable behind those glasses bathed with the reflection of a barely warming sun, Clara began to narrate the story she had prepared, polished, edited, and censored; the acceptable story for a son who needed to reconcile a mother who had abandoned him in a state of suspended animation, a to be—not to be the son of.

"This place was important to Sylvia. When she was little, her dad brought her here most every Sunday. He'd talk to her about the animals and the countries they came from, teach her to observe them, and at the end of the afternoon, he bought her a Vascolet . . . it was a kind of cocoa," she clarified at the uncomprehending looks of the young people—oh, how can anyone be that young! really! "—and an alfajor cookie. They'd sit down on these benches, facing the swans, and Sylvia would ask her dad why they couldn't stay there like that, arm in arm, forever. He'd hug her a little closer and she would cry because it would soon be time to return home, to Laura's harshness, to the vomiting with which she sealed each Sunday, as an echo to her mother's piercing criticisms. It seemed as if the hours Sylvia spent with her father, Laura spent collecting phrases. *"Look how you've gotten your new shoes dirty," "your father has no sense at all, letting you have an alfajor before dinner."* That's how she welcomed her back, with few variations, each and every Sunday of her childhood. Sylvia would rush to the bathroom; Laura would lock herself in her study. Pulling herself together, still sobbing, Sylvia would dial her father's number. But he wasn't there . . . when he wasn't with her he vanished into the city, out of her reach until their next meeting. And Laura took advantage of the opportunity to rub it in: *"Look at the sort of father you have. Who knows where he goes off to, what sort of people he hangs around with."* And so forth and so on. I didn't know your grandfather but apparently it never occurred to Laura that she was the one who had chosen Sylvia's father. She talked about him as if he was just some guy who had crossed her path by pure coincidence.

As a teenager she no longer saw her father on the weekends, but she often came to the zoo on her own, to sketch the animals. She'd spend hours in front of the more open spaces: she was fascinated by the harts. She filled several sketchbooks with wonderful drawings of harts.

Clara had gradually forgotten she was not alone. She turned to glare at them abruptly as if wondering what they were doing there. She sighed, conceding that in reality she was talking for them, for Lucas, and asked him, a little ashamed:

"Do you have them? The sketchbooks?"

"I didn't even know Mom liked to draw. There was nothing like that. As far as I know, there never was." Lucas never ceased to be amazed. Who, what had his mother been when she wasn't his mother? Was this what she had wanted to tell him about?"

"She probably threw them out," reflected Clara. "She always ended up throwing out the parts of her life she considered 'over and done with'."

"Just toss the ashes," murmured Lucas.

"What?" Clara and Estela, in unison.

"Something Mom wrote. It doesn't matter. Go on."

Clara embarked on a parenthesis on the matter of throwing out. She'd been over it with Sylvia so many times, trying to convince her that some day she'd regret this systematic throwing out with no possibility of recovery. The last time, not long before her death, Sylvia had smiled the very peculiar smile of hers, without parting her lips the slightest bit. She'd said: *"Other people save things on my behalf, if not for me."* In response to Clara's look of exasperated bewilderment, she'd added: *"All of you, my friends, save photographs and videos in which I appear, the letters and postcards I've written you; Silvina, poor thing, has even saved my notebooks from primary school. It's fine, if you all want those keepsakes. But beggars get around better without keepsakes."*

"She made me jump out of my chair," Clara confessed to a teary-eyed Lucas and an open-mouthed, completely lost Estela.

"She . . ." Lucas pulled himself together, "she had these things. They appeared in stuff she'd write when she was feeling really bad, or she'd yell them at Dad. It gave you goose bumps."

Estela squeezed his hand tightly. In their private code, she transmitted that all of that was over now and it was useless to stir it all up.

Lucas responded aloud.

"I don't want to stir it all up. I just want to understand the bare minimum that will enable me to live with this dead mother."

"Okay, Lucas," Clara resumed her story. "I don't want to get ahead of myself, but perhaps it isn't so much a matter of understanding as accepting. You'll see. In any case, and to finish, this was the place she always chose when she needed to make a major decision. But she never came back again on a Sunday. She said it made her too sad. It wasn't the same as before."

"She must have been thinking about her dad," affirmed Estela.

Clara gave her a hard look, tempered by the dark lenses. How was it that the simplest, not to mention naïve, people manage to hit the nail on the head so totally innocently? Although it was obvious really. Estela couldn't possibly fathom the extremes to which Sylvia bled for her dad her whole life.

"So you didn't know my grandfather?" More than a question, it was just a search for confirmation of something Clara had already mentioned. It was within the rules; it was a rhetorical question Clara would not refuse to answer, thought Lucas, even as he posed it.

She picked up a stick and began to trace a strange figure in the moss at her feet. She seemed not to have heard. She was absorbed in her design. Finally as a cross began to take shape, framed by the Star of David, she addressed the expectant silence of her two companions.

"Just this one, Lucas," she warned him, "and only to clarify, because perhaps I didn't explain myself very well. What I meant to say was I did not have any relationship with him. I saw your grandfather on a couple of occasions. He was a good guy, exceedingly self-contained. Your mom adored him."

"Mom almost never mentioned him. Isn't that strange?" But he, Lucas, had not wanted to hear his mom's stories either. Would that be what . . . ?

"In a way, although two very different people, your grandfather and your dad were similar. In their way of facing the world I mean. In that they devoted their energy to living, whatever that meant. Sylvia told me that when your grandfather was very ill, he made plans to take her out to dinner at a very trendy restaurant. He lasted only two days after that. And until the last second, he was convinced he was going to get well . . . Your mom too, even though the doctors had made it crystal clear to them that it was the end. It was a horrendous shock. It was very difficult to get her past it."

" 'If you believe, it exists.' Isn't that what your mom always said, Lucky?" Estela recalled. "How could she go on with that if her dad's death had shown her things didn't work that way?"

"No, Estela; she didn't say it for herself; she said it for me. She, poor thing, didn't even believe the day was a day."

Conscious that it was getting chillier as the shadows dimmed the lake's radiance, Lucas offered to take Clara home.

"Thanks, Lucky, but I'm going to stay a little longer. You two go on. Sylvia spent so much time here that I feel closer to her here than in other places. And it does me good. Go on then. See you soon."

After the goodbye kisses, walking along the wide, windswept avenue, a now familiar thought took hold inside Lucas, urging him to resign himself, "she doesn't even have a grave."

Chapter X

2010

In the bar of the Hotel Sheraton in New York, a woman between sixty and seventy years old—it was difficult to tell exactly, turned a demitasse of coffee between her carefully manicured hands. The pale gold highlights tinting her white hair illuminated the tan foundation spread over a discreet plastic surgery that had erased the more excessive marks of time. The green eyes traced with dark eyeliner returned over and over again to the reception area, straining to identify a face, a form, that she'd taken it upon herself to come visit . . . although she was no longer certain why. Of what significance could it be to them, to him and to her, such a brief reunion after so many years during which they'd even seemed to be avoiding each other? When he, recently married, had moved to New York, he had not said goodbye or left an address. She'd traveled a couple of times accompanying her husband, with the telephone number obtained through a long list of interlocutors, but she'd never called. He had returned to Buenos Aires on occasion, always for just a couple of days: to put the office up for sale when Francisco decided to leave having accepted an offer from a Mexico-based human rights group; to reinstall his father, along with his new wife, in what had been the family home; to accompany Estela's family when the grandmother had passed away. His mother's friends would find out about the visit following his departure through intermediaries who had seen him, or thought they had anyway.

Increasingly uncomfortable as the minutes passed, Sofía was wondering whether it wouldn't make more sense to go, to leave the past in the past.

But now a tall, well-dressed man with short dark hair and a penetrating look was moving toward her, both hands extended. Automatically Sofía reached out with hers and was trapped in the firm grip of long, finely shaped fingers. She noted without surprise that his warmth enveloped her and that a deep vertical line transected his brow.

Finally, the hands released her and Lucas sat down beside her smiling mirthlessly.

"Have you come alone? What would you like to drink? I was hoping to see Estela and the girls . . ." Sofía could not stop talking and Lucas made no effort to stop her. He also would have preferred to avoid this encounter, but Estela had made him accept.

"You can't always escape, Lucky. What can be so bad about an old friend of your mom's wanting to catch up with you a bit?"

"You know very well that I finished my tour of my mother's haunts ten years ago. For me, those paths are closed off."

"Lucas! Stop talking like a character out of an Argentine soap opera. The poor woman would like to see you. And if you think getting together with a friend of your mother's is going to cause problems, then you already have a problem. Come on. Call her and fix yourself up."

Lucas conceded. It was hard not to in the face of the monument of common sense that was his wife.

"Okay, but you come with me."

"No go. I only set eyes on the woman once in my entire life. I don't want her to feel as if you've brought your bodyguards."

She'd caught him out, as usual. Estela's presence would have guaranteed general topics and a quick goodbye.

"Okay, wise one. I'll do it for you. But I warn you, I'm going to make you pay."

"Oh come on! You're scaring me now. Uy, Lucky, look at the time! The girls will be home from school and I haven't even started dinner. Help me out, will you? Bring the lettuce for the salad . . ."

Into this stable, organized life, Estela's unswerving attachment to Earth and to the advantages of the Mother Country (America, Ameericaa . . .), Lucas had established his talent as a graphic designer, as well as a typical, ordinary family. He did not want his present to be tainted by outbursts from the past.

"You haven't changed, Sofía. You're as beautiful as always," he said seriously.

"Oh Lucky! Aren't you sweet! Did you bring pictures at least? Let's see, show me . . ."

Lucas barely shook his head.

"I'm not much into pictures. Estela's the one who lives with a camera hanging around her neck, like most people here."

"Just like your mother. She detested photographs and, on top of that, she threw them out. She said they were printed lies to sell some illusion of reality.

Lucas was not willing to take the walk down memory lane, much less by way of comparisons.

"Tell me, Sofía, did you want to see me for any particular reason?" he stopped her in her tracks.

"Yes. No. I don't know. Someone's always talking about . . . who takes a trip and brings back news . . . through someone who saw you . . .". Sofía was getting tangled up; he made no move to help her. Everyone knew Lucas only stayed in touch with his own friends in Buenos Aires, and his friends did not belong to his mother's circle of acquaintances. Of course, his father knew how to locate him, but they didn't communicate very often. Jaime claimed to be in his second youth and was reveling in it. He divided his time between administering his wife's beauty parlor and his recently discovered passion for tango. He communicated sporadically with his grand-daughters by e-mail. They called him "the crazy grandpa"; peek-a-boo, now you see him now you don't.

Cutting short his musings, Lucas decided to extend a verbal hand to the babbling Sofía who couldn't seem to get out whatever it was she'd come to say. Or had come not to say? Why did he have the feeling that those who had been close to his mother had taken it upon themselves to surround her with walls, in addition to those other ones he'd never succeeded in penetrating? Weren't the walls Sylvia herself had erected enough?

"Okay Sofía. So what is it they're saying, hm?"

"That you're doing very well; that you have a wonderful family . . ."

"That's true. And you wanted to see it with your own eyes? So you could rest easier? After ten years?"

He couldn't stop himself. The cut went deep. He hadn't received any pity, why dole it out?

"No, Lucas." Sofía forced herself not to cry in front of the spoiled little brat, just as Francisco had described him the interminable night of Sylvia never more. "No," Sofía repeated. "Actually, I came to bring you something." And in a second, she had deposited on the table a small bundle wrapped in tissue paper. "Come on now; open it."

Lucas took it with some apprehension, without taking his eyes off her, hoping to discern the nature of the object in her eyes before exposing it to the light. But her eyes were wells of sadness, their shiny green dulled, they only transmitted pain and not for him. Spoiled brat.

Lucas ripped the paper and laid it aside. The shape of the object blended into the streaked marble, but even so he knew. The thing that had been missing, had been forgotten. A useless relic registered as lost and never searched for.

"It's Mom's watch. I don't understand. What are you doing with Mom's watch?"

The watch, cheap and simple, was working perfectly and time leaped crazily backwards, stopping suddenly on days Lucas had disowned. *"If you don't believe, it doesn't exist."*

"Sylvia was at my house . . . Saturday afternoon. No. Let me speak, because if I don't say it all at once I'm not going to be able to. It took me ten years to get my courage up. Now then, she was at my house. Watching some videos we'd rented. Juan had gone out to play golf. But she had something else on her mind. I asked her. She told me she was trying to make a decision. She said if she didn't make it, 'things were going to become impossible.' 'What things? Let me help you,' I said. I kept insisting but she just withdrew into herself; you know how she was when she didn't want something. She spent several hours with her mind somewhere off in the distance . . . Then her face relaxed, she seemed content. 'You've figured it out,' I asked her. She said yes she had. And I responded that I was glad. How horrible! I was glad. And she went to wash her hands, gathered her things, and said goodbye. I went into the bathroom before accompanying her down. 'You forgot your watch,' I said. 'It doesn't matter. I won't be needing it,' she answered. And she left. And I thought that finally she was going to buy a decent watch." Sofía laughed, cried, shook Lucas by the shoulders. "I kept it so we could laugh about it together later, about how crazy she was, all those years wearing that trashy watch, the proud Ms. Meyer, attorney at law. And then on Monday Estela called. I'd been glad, do you realize Lucas? She had found the solution and I had been glad!"

Gently Lucas freed himself from Sofía's grip and glanced apologetically at the few customers at other tables. In the Mother Country, public scenes made one uncomfortable.

"Now I would have to ask you why I didn't know this before."

Lucas was aware that, during the journey on which he had embarked in the aftermath of his mother's death, he had skipped Sofía station. After listening to so many versions, so many back and forths, he had been overcome by a sort of mental fatigue. The more he delved, the less he understood. Ultimately it had become a cost benefit analysis. He had gained the conviction that he'd had the mother fate had assigned him. It was possible to love her in memory, at times, erase her from memory, at times, plunge into the rough terrain of the conditional "if," ineffectual and infinite, at times. He thought he had lost his passion for hate. It wasn't such a bad trade-off.

"I want you to have it, Lucas. To have something from Sylvia. I know you gave everything away. I think the struggle did you in, but this was salvaged. Call it a miracle, a mystery, whatever you like. This watch kept time for your mother and I kept it, marking the time she gave up. Take it, please."

Lucas kissed her lightly on the cheek and stood up.

"That isn't my time, Sofía, nor is it yours. It's nobody's. It's just time. Ciao. My best to Juan."

He didn't look back on the way to the door, the street, the corner. He shook his jacket to shake off those green eyes, darkened in a reproach he did not accept. *So far, Sylvia, we're getting along just fine.*

THE END

The Author

RESUME

Marta Inés Merajver (Marta Castillo) graduated as translator from the School of Economics, Buenos Aires University, in the 60s. She also holds a Diploma of English Studies from Cambridge University (England) and a General Certificate of Education (London University, England). She has trained in Psychology and Psychoanalysis at the School of Psychology, Buenos Aires University.

Ms Merajver has shared her time between lecturing and translation.

Between 1970 and 1983 she held the chairs of Contemporary Literature and Drama, Theoretical Linguistics, Literary Translation, Simultaneous Translation and Advanced Language at the Asociación Argentina de Cultura Inglesa in Buenos Aires.

For the ensuing five years, she was appointed Head of the Technical English Department and of the English Teacher-Training College at ORT ARGENTINA.

She resigned to take over the Department of International Examinations at BAE Center, Buenos Aires, and in 1991 was appointed exclusive representative—in Argentina and Uruguay—of G-TELP (General Tests of English Language Proficiency) by SDSU's College of Extended Studies, and Educational Consultant to UCLA's College of Extended Studies.

Over the past eight years, she has been a guest lecturer at Escuela Freudiana de Buenos Aires. Since 2004, she has held the chair of English and American Literature for Psychoanalysts at the said Institution.

Among her translations, she would like to mention the following:

REWARDS FOR KIDS, by Virginia Shiller PhD (Into Spanish, in progress)

TRAMA 2004—IMAGES, NARRATIVES AND UTOPIAS (Into English, to be published by Proyecto Trama—Fundación Espigas within the current year)

TRAMA 2002—IMAGES, NARRATIVES AND UTOPIAS (Into English, published by Proyecto Trama—Fundación Espigas, Buenos Aires, 2003)

DEL DI TELLA A "TUCUMAN ARDE", by Ana Longoni & Mariano Mestman (Into English, 2002, Goethe Institut, Buenos Aires)

CRITICAL VIEWS OF SEPTEMBER 11 (Into Spanish, commissioned by The Social Science Research Council, New York, for Siglo XX, Spain, 2002–2003)

UNDERSTANDING SEPTEMBER 11 (Into Spanish, commissioned by The Social Science Research Council, New York, for Siglo XX, Spain, 2002–2003)

LA TEORIA FEMINISTA Y EL DISCURSO JURIDICO, by Carol Smart (Into Spanish, in EL DERECHO EN EL GENERO Y EL GENERO EN EL DERECHO, Editorial Biblos, Buenos Aires, 2000)

NOT WAVING, by Gen LeRoy (Play, 1998, into Spanish, commissioned by copyright owner in Argentina Jorge Maestro, not staged because of contractual disagreements between Mr. Maestro and author's representatives)

CONFERENCIAS CLINICAS SOBRE KLEIN Y BION, Robin Anderson, compilador (Into Spanish, Editorial Paidós, Buenos Aires, 1991)

EDUCANDO A RITA, by Willy Russell (Into Spanish; staged in Buenos Aires by Alejandra Boero, 1989)

ENCICLOPEDIA DEL TOPO GIGIO (12 volumes, into Spanish, a publication to aid children's bilingual education in Latin America, Buenos Aires, Cuántica Editora, 1975–1977)

GEOCIENCIA (In collaboration, 4 volumes, into Spanish, Buenos Aires, Cuántica Editora, 1978)

HISTORIA DE LA REVOLUCION NORTEAMERICANA, by Herbert Aptheker (Into Spanish, Editorial Futuro, 1965)

Her private translation work includes academic papers by American Professors Eric Hershberg, Paul Gootenberg, Jeremy Aldeman, Mary Shanley, Eric Cantor and others, as well as for Argentinean psychoanalysts Roberto Harari, Isidoro Vegh, Alba Flessler, Daniel Paola, etc.